Forever Mine

Warn your people not to disturb you then settle in and start reading this phenomenal, heartfelt, swoony romance today! Your romantic heart will thank you.

— BOOKADDICT

The Prince I Love to Hate

The Prince I Love To Hate is an absolute must read! This romcom will have you rooting for Niamh and Olivier right from their hilarious first meeting.

— HARLEQUIN BOOK JUNKIE BLOG

Oopsie Daisy

Quirky, fun, witty, hilarious! Iris Morland always manages to get me to laugh out loud.

— WHISPERING CHAPTERS

He Loves Me, He Loves Me Not

A hilarious, sexy and heartwarming romantic comedy...you do not want to miss this fun, feel-good romance.

— MARY DUBÉ, CONTEMPORARILY EVER AFTER

...refreshing, funny, emotionally charged, and very entertaining to read.

— CAROL, TIL THE LAST PAGE

There is humor, there is heart and there is heat in this story! I absolutely loved it! . . . Mari and Liam delivered. Yowza, their chemistry was palpable.

— BIBLIOPHILE CHLOE

PETAL PLUCKER

Funny, charming, and utterly captivating! I devoured this sparkling read.

— ANNIKA MARTIN, NEW YORK TIMES BESTSELLING AUTHOR

Petal Plucker was funny, entertaining, fresh and fan-yourself-worthy . . . Their enemies-to-lovers romance is both charming, tender and steamy, and you'll love both of these characters (and their families!) and their sigh-worthy happily ever after.

— MARY DUBÉ, CONTEMPORARILY EVER AFTER

Morland has created a masterpiece of a romance . . . one of my favorite [books] of the year.

— CRISTIINA READS

Humorous, raunchy, and refreshing, Petal Plucker has rightfully earned its way, in my opinion, as one of the best romantic comedy [books] this year.

— CAROL, TIL THE LAST PAGE

My One and Only

This book was gripping, well written & the chemistry between the characters sizzled throughout this wonderful read.

— AMAZON REVIEW

All I Want Is You

Another heartfelt, steamy, terrific story. This is an author who really knows how to create a story that catches a reader's attention and characters that capture her heart.

— BOOKADDICT

TAKING A CHANCE ON LOVE

Thea and Anthony are in for a surprise when it comes to the language of the heart . . . I am in awe.

— HOPELESS ROMANTIC BLOG

THEN CAME YOU

This story really pulled all my heartstrings. This was truly a beautiful story and makes you believe there really is true love out there.

— MEME CHANELL BOOK CORNER

ALSO BY IRIS MORLAND

LOVE EVERLASTING

including

HAZEL ISLAND

One Perfect Summer

Forever Mine

My Heart to Keep

THE YOUNGERS

Then Came You

Taking a Chance on Love

All I Want Is You

My One and Only

THE THORNTONS

The Nearness of You

The Very Thought of You

If I Can't Have You

Dream a Little Dream of Me

Someone to Watch Over Me

Till There Was You

I'll Be Home for Christmas

THE HEIR AFFAIR DUET

The Prince I Love to Hate

The Princess I Hate to Love

HERON'S LANDING

Say You're Mine

All I Ask of You

Make Me Yours

Hold Me Close

THE FLOWER SHOP SISTERS

War of the Roses

Petal Plucker

He Loves Me, He Loves Me Not

Oopsie Daisy

MY HEART TO KEEP

HAZEL ISLAND

IRIS MORLAND

BLUE VIOLET PRESS LLC

My Heart to Keep
Copyright © 2022 by Iris Morland
Published by Blue Violet Press LLC
Seattle, Washington

Cover design by Qamber Designs

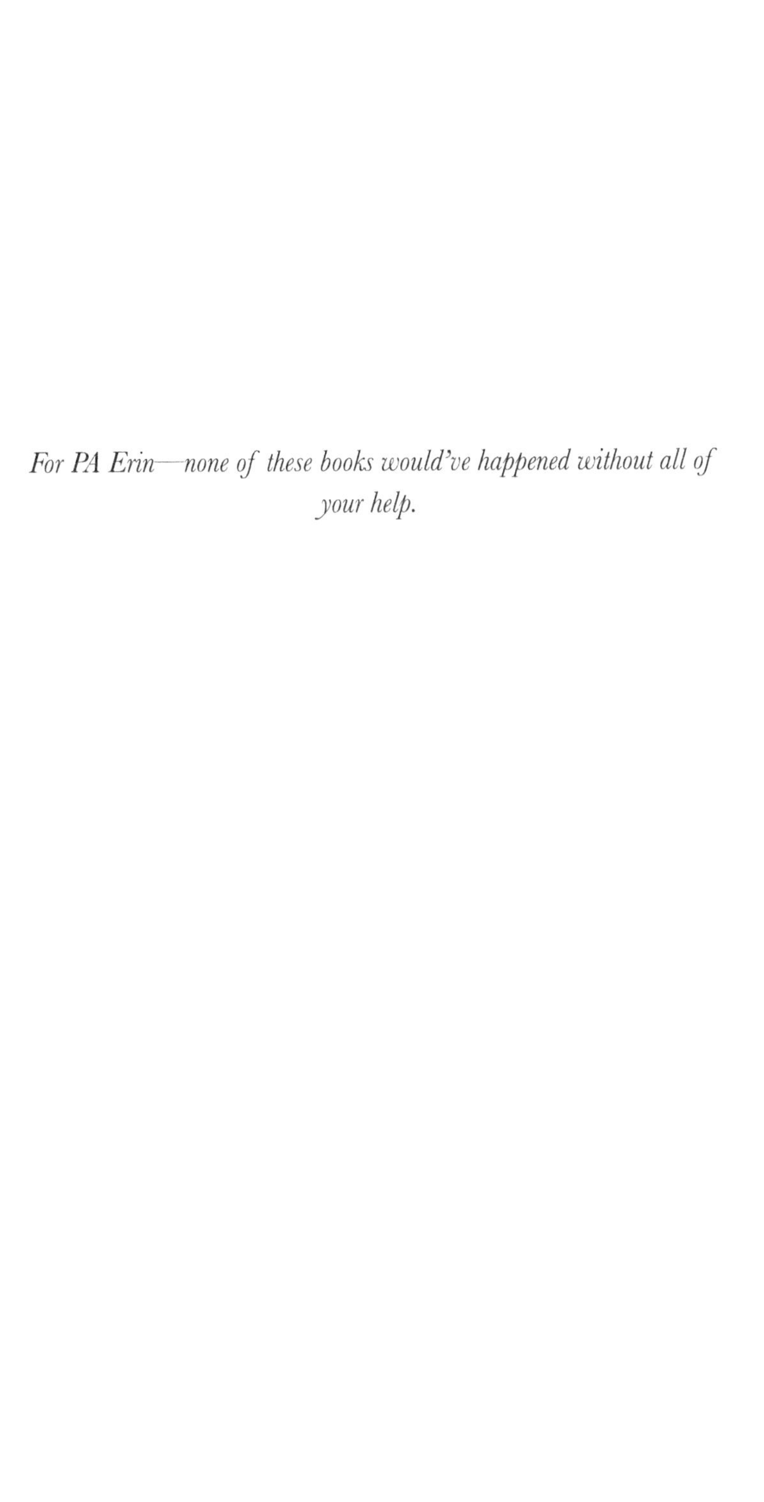

*For PA Erin—none of these books would've happened without all of
your help.*

MY HEART TO KEEP

Luke Wright loved the woods. He'd been lucky, growing up near woods he could wander around in to his heart's content. He'd only gotten lost once; after that, he'd always been careful about staying on the trails. He knew the trails near his parents' place like the back of his hand.

So when he heard a voice up ahead, he paused. This particular trail was on private property. Some of the trails were open to residents of Hazel Island, but not this one. It ran only a quarter mile from the Wright mansion, a meandering trail that was relatively flat.

Sometimes people who didn't know this trail was on private property wandered onto it. Although there were signs, people sometimes didn't heed them. Or didn't see them. Most people apologized and left without causing a ruckus.

When Luke realized the intruder was none other than his ultimate nemesis, he knew a ruckus was about to start.

Jocelyn Gray—nothing about her was gray or muted.

She was made of bright colors: red, like her temper, and the sharp side of her tongue that could make the thickest of hides bleed.

Yellow, like her golden hair that Luke already knew was silky soft. Blue, like her eyes and the heart of a flame.

Jocelyn was staring at her phone. When she heard Luke approach, her head whipped up. Then her eyes narrowed.

"Seriously?" was all she said before sighing loudly.

"Most people say the word 'hello.' Or 'hi.' I heard those are both acceptable greetings in the English language," he replied.

Jocelyn scoffed. "I have plenty of greetings I'd like to give you."

She was dressed for hiking, at least, so this trip wasn't impulsive. She had a water bottle, now three-quarters full. She was a little red-faced, but that might've just been because she was near Luke.

Luke was used to Jocelyn's antagonism aimed solely at him. She'd had her claws out, ready to scoop out his heart, since they'd been teenagers. And he couldn't exactly say that her reaction was unwarranted, either.

Luke stepped close enough that he could see a blush darkening on her cheeks. She pushed a few strands of hair from her forehead.

"Are you lost?" he said.

"No."

"Are you sure? You seem a little frustrated."

That made her snort. "I'm always frustrated."

"Fair point."

While Jocelyn continued to do whatever it was she was doing on her phone, he took in her appearance. She looked tired: the circles under her eyes were darker than usual. She also looked a bit thinner. Considering she was a chef, it was hard to imagine she wasn't getting enough to eat.

Her sharp gaze landed straight on his face. "Are you staring at me?"

"Yes. Does it bother you?"

"Obviously." Then she asked, "So? Have you figured me out yet?"

"No, but you do look tired."

He probably would've been better off telling her that she had nice tits than saying something that pointed out any vulnerability. She scowled darkly up at him.

"People who have to work for a living get tired," she snapped. She stuffed her phone into her pocket. "But you wouldn't know anything about that, would you?"

That smarted. Luke might come from a rich family, but he wasn't rich. He had to work, too. Maybe it wasn't a grueling, twelve-hour-shift kind of job that Jocelyn was used to, but he was hardly lazy.

"You know what they say about making assumptions," he said. "They're usually wrong. You have no idea what you're talking about."

Jocelyn just shrugged a shoulder. "Yet I'm sure you'll be fine regardless. Rich boys usually are."

As she began to walk in the direction of the Wright house, Luke considered telling her that she was on the wrong trail. But pettiness won that battle. He smiled, his teeth flashing, as he watched her firm backside flex ahead of him.

He started walking a few paces behind her. After about

three minutes, she said over her shoulder, "Are you stalking me?"

"We're just going in the same direction, that's all."

She narrowed her eyes at him. Then she shrugged and kept walking.

They were silent the rest of the way. When Jocelyn tripped on a rock, though, Luke shot forward to catch her. But she batted his hands away. "I'm fine," she said.

Would anyone convict me if I tossed this woman off the nearest cliff? he thought to himself. It was like being near a neurotic porcupine.

The trees thinned out as they got closer to the house. Jocelyn slowed a little, allowing Luke to catch up. "This isn't right," she said.

Luke said nothing. But as they got closer, the gates of the Wright house now in view, he could see Jocelyn's color rise in her face with every step.

He had to bite the inside of his cheek to keep from laughing. He knew if he made a sound, she'd go for his jugular. It'd probably be worth it, though. It wasn't too often he'd seen Jocelyn out of sorts like this.

She stopped walking a few yards from the gate. She began to fiddle with her phone as Luke waited. He'd wait all day and night if he had to.

Finally, Jocelyn put her phone away. Then she said in a tight voice, "Can you give me a ride to my car?"

When Luke stopped the car to let Jocelyn out, he locked the passenger door with the child lock mechanism before she could escape.

"Don't you have something to say to me?" he said sweetly.

If looks could kill, hers would have. Her expression just made Luke's grin grow wider.

"I guess I was lost after all," she muttered.

"No, not that."

Jocelyn was practically shaking. "You son of a bitch—"

"Come on, Gray. It's two words."

She looked like she might burst into flames. Or punch an elbow through his car window. Nothing would surprise him with Jocelyn Gray.

Then, to his surprise, she laughed. Laughed! The sound startled him because he'd so rarely heard it in his presence.

She shook her head, smiling wryly. "Thank you. You have saved me from an uncertain fate, kind sir."

He bowed. "You're welcome, my lady."

She snorted, got into her car, and was soon out of sight.

As LUKE WATCHED his parents out of the corner of his eye, he had to restrain a smile. Not because he was happy, exactly. There wasn't much to be happy about, considering this was the reading of his grandmother's will. He missed Granny Esther terribly.

But to see his dad squirming in his seat, when Gregory Wright had never squirmed in his entire life, was certainly memorable.

His mom, Juliet, stroked her latest Pomeranian. Luke couldn't remember its name. Its tongue was hanging out, and it looked like it had a grand total of three brain cells to rub together. This morning, Luke had watched the fluffy idiot bark madly at one of the fountains outside.

Granny's lawyer, Mr. Hitchens, was shuffling papers, muttering under his breath as he tried to get himself organized. Luke had a feeling the man was just stalling for time.

I wish Tristan were here, Luke thought. But his prodigal little brother hadn't shown his face at their parents' house in over a decade.

Hitchens cleared his throat. "Okay, yes, here we go." He cleared his throat a second time. "Mrs. Walter Wright changed her will six months prior to her death. These are the changes included herein."

Luke sat forward in his seat. So did his parents. Even the dog seemed to perk up its ears in anticipation.

"'All of my assets and money shall go to my grandson, Luke Gregory Wright. To my grandson Tristan Julian Wright, he shall inherit the remaining ten percent of Mrs. Walter Wright's money. My son, Gregory Kenneth Wright, and his wife, Juliet Rebecca Wright née Havens, shall receive nothing.'"

Luke had never understood the phrase "so silent you could hear a pin drop," but in that moment, it applied. It was as if a blanket of silence had covered the entire room. His heart was pounding so loudly, though, he was half-certain everyone could hear it.

"Are you fucking *kidding me?*" Luke's dad launched himself from his chair, causing the dog to start barking and jumping at his ankles. "That can't be the will. Is this a joke?"

Luke also stood up. He caught the dog before Gregory could kick it into the next galaxy. Gregory had never been cruel to his wife's pets, but this wasn't a usual moment. Luke stroked the dog until its barks turned into soft whimpers.

"Hitchens, can we see the will ourselves?" said Luke. He needed to see the paper it was written on, feel it under his fingertips. Maybe then all of this would seem real.

Hitchens cleared his throat for the third time. "I'm afraid to say I haven't finished reading it all. Please, take your seats."

Gregory, red-faced and steam nearly coming from his nostrils, didn't sit down. Luke handed the dog to his mom and wiped the dog hair from his shirt in vain.

"'Contingent upon inheriting, my grandson Luke Wright must fall in love and marry a suitable woman of his choice within one year of my death. He must stay married for three years,'" recited Hitchens.

Now it was Luke's turn to say, "Are you serious? Please tell me you aren't serious."

Fall in love and marry? He'd always known Granny was eccentric, and even overbearing, but this was insane.

"'My dearest friend Opal Johnson will meet with Luke and his wife to determine if they are in love upon marriage. If she sees that he is trying to skirt the rules, she will inform my lawyer and provide documentation of her findings.'" Hitchens pulled at his collar, looking uncomfortable.

That was when Luke started laughing. He knew he sounded hysterical. The entire situation *was* hysterical. Granny Esther must be laughing her bony little ass off wherever she was, damn the woman.

"And what about my brother?" said Luke suddenly.

"It says here that he must return to Hazel Island within a year and live here for three years to inherit," replied Hitchens.

"This is outrageous!" Gregory slammed a hand onto the

desk, making Hitchens jump and the dog bark again. He grabbed the papers from Hitchens, reading over the text and turning redder and redder. "This can't be real," he kept saying over and over.

Juliet, for her part, was the only one who seemed calm. But Luke could tell she was upset, too. She wasn't petting the dog but instead chewing on her bottom lip. She only ever did that when she was really agitated, because she hated messing up her lipstick otherwise.

"Listen to this," said Gregory, his expression sneering. "'As I loved my dearest David, I want the same for my eldest grandson. As far as my younger grandson, I want him to return to his home and reunite with his family. These two things, I wish for with all my heart.' What a bunch of bullshit!"

Despite himself, the image of Jocelyn in a wedding gown, walking toward him, burst into Luke's mind. He pushed the thought ruthlessly away. *There's been enough insanity for today*, he reminded himself.

Luke took the papers from his dad's grip as Gregory started pacing like a caged tiger. Even reading the words himself didn't make them seem real.

Luke was tempted to say to hell with the money. Even Granny didn't have the right to dictate who he married. But Luke had been counting on inheriting a substantial amount of money that wouldn't just be for his own enjoyment. It would be hugely beneficial to so many people.

Luke's mind started turning, trying to find a way out of this. But deep down, he knew Granny would've made sure he couldn't wriggle out of this. Wily to her last days was Esther Wright.

"Granny did always like a good joke," said Luke.

At that, his dad whirled on him, pointing a finger in his face. "You! You did this. You influenced her. You went behind my back and made her change the will. There was no reason she would've done this to me. I was her only son. I took care of her, paid for her to be in the nicest facility, got her the best nurses, all of it. And she repays me like this!"

Luke pushed his dad's hand aside. "Do you honestly think I could've gotten Granny to do anything she didn't want to do? Come on."

Gregory scowled. He knew Luke was right. No one had been as stubborn as Granny. Even in the moment before she'd breathed her last, she'd reminded her son that she'd wanted her body to be cremated. If he didn't heed her wishes, she'd come back to haunt him. No one in the family had ever been cremated; the Wrights had the largest cemetery plot on Hazel Island. But Granny had wanted to defy tradition just like she always had.

"Well, this has been a little too much excitement for me." Juliet stood. She came over to kiss Luke's cheek. In a whisper, she said to Luke, "Better avoid your dad for now. I don't want any bloodshed ruining my brand-new carpets."

Luke just chuckled darkly and did as he was told for once.

CHAPTER TWO

T he one downside to being a chef, Jocelyn had realized early on, was that when she got home, she didn't want to cook for herself. She'd never admit to anyone that she often microwaved a Hot Pocket or made a pot of macaroni and cheese from the infamous blue box most nights. Other times, she took home leftovers from the restaurant, so at least in that way, she was eating something she cooked herself.

But for other people? She'd always cook for them. She'd more than once wondered what that said about her, but she didn't exactly have money for therapy to figure it out.

After making a plate of homemade lasagna and salad for her dad, she made one for herself. She carried both plates to the living room where Pete Gray spent most of his days.

Pete was watching *Wheel of Fortune*, which he watched every evening.

"It's 'scuba diving and snorkeling'!" he said to the TV.

"Did this guy seriously just guess one of the letters was an 'x' when there are two letters left?"

Jocelyn handed her dad his plate. "It'd be pretty embarrassing to choke when the answer is that obvious."

"I should've been on this show." This was something Pete said at least once a week. He'd even tried to get on the show in his younger years, but it'd never worked out. Now, he was too ill to leave his recliner, let alone fly to California.

In his early sixties, Pete Gray looked at least ten years older. A tall, thin man, his hair had disappeared before he'd turned age thirty. Growing up, Jocelyn had always seen him with a beard. But the last few years, Pete had started shaving again. His beard grew in random patches. He always joked that this new type of beard made it seem like he kept shaving his face in the dark with a Swiss army knife.

Pete had been the only parent Jocelyn and her younger sister Alexandra had ever known. Their mom had walked out of their lives when they'd been just kids.

"Is this from the restaurant?" said Pete as he ate the lasagna.

"Nope, made it fresh today and brought it over for you."

Pete made a tsking sound. "You don't need to cook for me, Jossy. I know you're busy. I'm fine eating a turkey sandwich or noodles."

"Like I'm going to let you eat ramen noodles." Jocelyn pointed at his untouched salad. "Eat your veggies."

He just snorted, but he did as she asked. He usually did, especially now that he was unlikely to fully recover from his last stroke.

Jocelyn couldn't help but watch as he struggled to lift his fork to his mouth; how slack the right side of his face had remained. He struggled to remember basic details, and Jocelyn had noticed that he often talked about the same five things over and over again. After months of physical therapy, he'd been able to walk again with the assistance of a walker. Not being able to walk easily, though, still frustrated her dad.

He couldn't run anymore. He couldn't drive and doing much beyond microwaving a bowl of ramen noodles was beyond him. Where once he'd seemed so *alive*, now he just seemed diminished.

His poor health was why Jocelyn had moved in with him when she'd returned to Hazel Island nearly two years ago. Although Alex helped as much as she could, she had her own business to run that occupied much of her time.

But despite his body failing him, Pete's mind was still there. Maybe it wasn't as sharp as it had been, but the essentials of Pete Gray were in there. For that, Jocelyn was thankful.

"How are things at the restaurant? You've been working a lot of hours," said Pete once they'd finished eating.

Along with her friend and boss, Gwen Parker, Jocelyn had opened a brand-new restaurant on Hazel Island called Lyn's Eatery. Jocelyn, a trained chef who'd attended culinary school in New York, had jumped at the chance to be the new head chef. Even if the restaurant was located on a tiny island in the Puget Sound.

"I'm still working on getting my staff up to speed," hedged Jocelyn.

Pete raised an eyebrow. "Having trouble?"

Jocelyn gritted her teeth. Her sous chef Kelly was talented, and she knew it. To the point that she acted like

Jocelyn giving her constructive criticism was offensive. Just yesterday, Jocelyn had taken Kelly aside to tell her that her knife cuts had been messy, and Kelly had not taken the comment well.

"Do you think I'm intimidating?" Jocelyn blurted.

Her dad, bless his heart, took a few moments to reply. "I think you're a strong woman who knows what she wants. To some people, that might be intimidating."

She smiled. "You mean I tend to run over people without even realizing it."

"Let's just say even I know not to get in your way." He winked.

But Jocelyn, despite her tough exterior, wasn't all that tough on the inside. She'd heard her staff whispering about her, complaining about how she was a hard-ass. *She got on me for being five minutes late. Why does she always have a stick up her ass?* one waiter said earlier that week when he thought Jocelyn wasn't listening. *She's not even our boss. Gwen is!*

Jocelyn had wanted to point out that she was the boss when Gwen wasn't around. And the waiter in question had been late multiple times now, and during their busiest times.

"I don't think any of my coworkers like me." She stretched her legs out on the ottoman, sighing. "I told myself I'd do better with this new job. Make nice, make friends. But then I see them wasting time, doing sloppy work, being little shitheads. And I can't make myself stay nice."

"You ever stop to think that you might have too high of standards for yourself?" said Pete quietly.

Jocelyn groaned. "Not this again."

"Sweetheart, you've always felt like you needed to be

perfect. The best student, the best chef. I'd tell you to relax, but I know you won't listen. But maybe cut your staff some slack. They're learning like you're learning."

Despite herself, Jocelyn pictured Luke Wright in her mind. If anyone thought she was a certifiable shithead, it was him. But she thought *he* was a shithead, so it was fine.

She was fine with Luke hating her. She'd had a long time to get used to the idea. Besides, she was pretty sure she was incapable of being nice to him at this point. He was so arrogant, so sure he was right, so good at getting under her skin with just a single passing comment.

Jocelyn got up to do the dishes, her mind turning. Why did she care so much what other people thought of her? She didn't need anyone's approval, except for her dad's. And she had that.

Why yearn for approval that didn't matter?

She cut up some carrots, gathering some other veggies to feed her rabbit, aptly named Fluffernutter. The rabbit was currently curled up on his little bed in her bedroom. When he saw her coming toward him with dinner, he stretched and yawned before doing his happy dance.

Jocelyn placed the veggies in his kennel, along with adding more pellets to his bowl. He kicked his back feet in excitement. A gray rabbit with a white eyepatch, Fluffer was basically like a dog in rabbit form. Or maybe more like a cat: he was litter trained, after all.

"You approve of me, don't you?" she said, petting the rabbit's silky ears.

Fluffer was currently occupied with eating. Jocelyn always smiled as she watched him nearly inhale the carrot and spinach she'd give him most nights.

Leaving Fluffer to his dinner, she returned to the kitchen. As she passed the kitchen table that was covered in mail, papers, and other random items, she picked up one of the bills with a red PAST DUE on the envelope.

She glanced at the living room, but her dad was watching some reality show. He'd be pissed that she'd read his mail. But when she took out the letter inside, she was glad she'd violated that promise.

It was a medical bill. It said that it'd go to collections if the bill wasn't paid immediately.

Her dad had assured her more than once that she didn't need to help him with his bills. She'd believed him, but she'd had her suspicions.

Jocelyn had been giving her dad money, assuming it'd gone toward his bills. So where was it going?

"Dad," she said, handing him the bills. "What are these?"

He didn't even blink. He took the envelopes and stuck them in the side of the recliner's cushion. "Nothing you need to worry about."

"Dad. Come on. You're not paying the mortgage? What's going on? You could go into foreclosure. You could lose the house—"

Pete put up a hand. "I told you: don't worry about it. I have it under control."

Jocelyn sat down, taking his hand. "You clearly don't. I thought I was giving you enough money. But I can give you more. I'll pay as much as I can."

"No. Absolutely not. You have your student loans to pay off. I'm your dad. I'm not asking you to give me any more money."

Jocelyn just waited. When Pete seemed to realize she wasn't going to let the subject go, he sighed.

"I wish I could tell you the money you've given me is going to something fun. Like gambling. Or cocaine," he said.

Jocelyn snorted. "You've never even smoked a cigarette, Dad."

"Never too late to try something new." His smile soon faded. "But I'm behind on everything. The medical bills, they keep piling up. Insurance is refusing to pay for the latest. I call and call, but it doesn't matter. They won't budge."

"I wish you would've told me."

He squeezed her hand. "I'm your dad. This is my responsibility, not yours."

"I can at least hound insurance for you. We already decided that I'm intimidating, right? I'll bully them into submission."

He chucked her under the chin. "I'm sure you could."

As Jocelyn lay in bed that night, she couldn't sleep. Her head was all numbers, wondering how she was going to make enough money to help her dad for real. As he'd said, she had student loans to repay. Although she wasn't paying rent, exactly, she had her own expenses. Her car, for one. Maybe she could sell that, but it wasn't worth much to begin with.

She'd taken a pay cut, starting this business with Gwen, and she'd been okay with it. Now, though, she almost wished she hadn't. There wasn't much left over at the end of the day, and Gwen wasn't in a position to offer Jocelyn a raise, either.

She could ask Alex, but she had her own money troubles. The bookstore she'd bought and ran was struggling.

Turning over, Jocelyn heard Fluffer climbing the stairs onto her bed. He snuggled down next to her, nosing her hand, as if asking her if she was okay.

"If only I was rich," she said to the rabbit. "If I were rich like Luke Wright, I could make this all go away. He's a lucky son of a bitch. Rich and handsome. While us peasants can barely pay our bills."

She sighed. If she saw Luke's annoying, handsome face in her dreams, she failed to mention it to anyone the following day. She might not have any money, but at least she had her pride.

CHAPTER THREE

"We're closing, you know," said an exasperated Jocelyn.

Luke looked up. He hadn't even noticed that Lyn's Eatery had emptied out. He looked at his watch. *Have I really been sitting here for three hours?*

"Shit," he mumbled. He finished off his beer and then placed a hundred dollar bill on the bar top. "Did the bartender leave? I need to tip her."

"I'll make sure she gets it." Jocelyn collected the cash and moved to open the register, but Luke stopped her.

"Keep the change. Give it to the bartender. Hell, take some for yourself. Get something nice."

Jocelyn frowned at him. She tended to do that. If she wasn't telling him off, shooting him dagger eyes, or frowning, Luke wasn't sure what he'd do with himself. If she ever smiled at him, he might collapse from the shock.

"You're drunk," said Jocelyn wonderingly.

"I'm mildly inebriated," he corrected.

She snorted. "So you're drunk. Do I need to drive you home?"

"I can walk home."

"It's three miles to your place, uphill. And it's dark."

"Worried about me falling to my death?"

Now she was really frowning. "More like you getting lost and then the entire island has to go out searching for you."

Luke considered her. She sounded annoyed, but did he detect a hint of concern? *You really are drunk.*

Jocelyn didn't show concern. He wasn't entirely sure the devil woman was capable of the feeling.

Despite himself, the memory of holding her in his arms returned. She'd kissed him like she'd wanted to kiss him for years. Decades. But then she'd reverted to her usual cold-hearted self when Jack Benson, Gwen's fiancé and Luke's best friend, had caught them in their embrace.

"I'm staying at my place," said Luke finally. "It's a short walk from here."

"Oh." Jocelyn was currently placing dirty glasses in a bin.

"You sound disappointed. Did you want to drive me home after all?"

She shot him a look that said she'd happily claw his balls off. "You have five minutes before I throw your ass out."

"That's not very good customer service."

"Like I said, we're closed. We've been closed for the better part of an hour."

"Then why are you still here?"

"None of your business."

When she carried the bin to the kitchen, Luke found himself following her. Was it because he liked to watch her ass bounce as she walked? Or how he'd like to imagine taking her blond hair from its tight bun, letting it fall down her back in soft waves?

No, of course not. He never, ever lusted after the one woman who hated his guts.

Lies, Wright, lies, he thought darkly.

Jocelyn set the bin next to the dishwasher, ignoring Luke. He watched as she began chopping onions with such speed that he couldn't help but be impressed.

When she started chopping some bell peppers, though, she was halfway through when she stopped with a curse.

"Shit, shit, shit," she kept saying as she went to the sink.

"Did you cut yourself?" said Luke.

"Did I get blood on the peppers? No, it doesn't matter. I'll have to throw them out anyway. Damn." She hissed as she let the cold water run over the cut on her left index finger.

"Where's your first-aid kit?" said Luke.

"In my office. On top of the cabinet. Wait, I'll show you—"

"I'll find it. You'll just drip blood all over your clean floor."

Luke had to restrain a chuckle when Jocelyn complied. She might not like him helping her, but he knew she'd hate to get blood everywhere.

He found the kit without issue, forcing himself not to stay longer to poke around her office. But damn if he wasn't curious. All he could see was that it was extremely neat. It almost looked like it was barely used at all.

When Luke returned, Jocelyn didn't say anything as he put on gloves and had her hold gauze against the cut.

"Press that hard," he said.

"Do you think I'll need stitches?"

"How deep was the cut? I know when I cut my hand, I went so deep that I saw bone."

Jocelyn whitened. Luke grabbed a nearby step stool just in the nick of time before her knees gave out.

"Put your head between your knees. Yes, like that. And breathe through your nose. Deep breaths." Luke squeezed her shoulder.

"Please don't talk about seeing bone," whispered Jocelyn.

"Noted."

Normally he would've been tempted to tease her, but at the moment, all he felt was anxiety. Seeing her sway like that, the blood draining from her cheeks… Seeing a woman who'd always seemed together be so vulnerable was terrifying.

He busied himself with getting her finger bandaged as he reminded her to breathe. When he checked the cut, the flow of blood had already slowed.

A few moments later, he was surreptitiously cleaning up the blood that had gotten onto the floor before pressing a glass of water into Jocelyn's hands. "Drink that."

She complied. When had Jocelyn ever done what he'd asked without protest? *She must really be out of it*, he thought.

She drank the water and slowly seemed to come back to herself. When she glanced at her finger, thick with bandages, she let out a snort. "Did you use an entire roll of gauze on it?"

"I probably went overboard. How's your head?"

"I'm okay." And then as if something in her brain was

reset, she stood up straight, hiding any weakness she might still be feeling. "I'm fine. You don't have to stay."

"You almost fainted."

"It's happened to me before. Blood, bad cuts…" She shuddered. "I've never fainted, but it makes me light-headed. One time when I was in Paris, one of my coworkers chopped off the tip of his finger. The chef did faint that time."

Luke gazed down at her. Jocelyn Gray wasn't conventionally attractive, but with her sharp little chin, her dark blue eyes, and her golden hair, she stood out. She'd always stood out to him. He'd known her since they were kids, yet at the same time, he felt like he'd never really *known* her.

He touched her cheek. When she didn't pull away, he exulted.

But then there was a noise—a raccoon getting into the garbage outside? But it was loud enough that it shattered the moment.

"You can go," repeated Jocelyn. Then, more softly, "Thank you."

"Did Jocelyn Gray really say the words 'thank you'?" He put a hand dramatically across his forehead. "Now I'm going to faint."

"And I won't keep you from falling on your head."

She was throwing out the peppers now, muttering under her breath. "I hate wasted food," she said, unprompted. "Especially because I was being clumsy."

Luke leaned against the counter. "You just can't be calm with me around. It's okay. I understand. I have that effect on women."

She pointed her knife at him. "Don't push your luck, Wright."

"Murder is illegal in all fifty states, I'm afraid."

"No jury would ever convict me."

He laughed at her. "Everyone in this town knows you hate me. I'm afraid you'd have a hell of a time convincing anyone you didn't murder me."

She had no reply to that. He chuckled as she did her best to ignore him, even though she kept having to go around him to place the bowls of chopped vegetables in the walk-in fridge.

"I don't hate you," said Jocelyn suddenly. Then, to Luke's surprise, she blushed. "I mean, I hate that you seem to enjoy annoying me all the time, but I don't actually want to murder you."

Luke stared at her. "Based on how you've acted around me, it seemed a whole lot like you hate me."

"It's complicated." Her gaze slanted toward his. "So why were you drinking tonight? I don't think I've ever seen you drunk."

He was about to tease her about paying attention to his drinking habits, but her question only brought up what had happened just this morning.

Luke had gone to his parents' place to talk about the will. The discussion, unfortunately, had quickly devolved into arguing. His dad had told him in no uncertain terms that if Luke didn't get married and inherit, he'd essentially be throwing his parents to the wolves.

"Have you ever once thought about your mom? Have you? If you don't give a shit about me, then at least think about her," said Gregory, disgust lacing his voice.

"Neither of you will starve," replied Luke.

But his mom, who was currently dabbing away tears, just sniffled. "We'll lose the house," she whispered. "All of the memories here. Most of our things. We can't pay for it without that money. We'd been counting on it."

Luke knew that. He also had had no reason to believe Granny would skip over his dad. She'd never so much as uttered a word about it. Then again, had she ever actually *said* Gregory would inherit? Luke couldn't remember.

"Do you want your mom to go find a job? To be the laughingstock of the island?" Gregory rubbed his temples, especially as Juliet began to cry more loudly.

Luke bit back the sharp reply sitting on his tongue. His mom had never worked a day in her life. He doubted she could get a job anywhere. She'd been raised to be a rich man's wife and raise a rich man's family. The idea of her folding clothes at some chain, using a cash register, answering phones? It was laughable because Luke knew his mom wouldn't last two days at a job like that.

"Who the hell should I marry, then? Because I don't exactly have a candidate available," Luke said.

"Find one. Any woman would jump at the chance to marry a Wright." Gregory smiled grimly. "Think of it as a scavenger hunt for a wife."

Luke had subsequently drowned himself in alcohol. His loyalty to his parents—really, to his mom—tugged at him. And he'd also been counting on receiving some of the money. He had plans to invest in the island's infrastructure, to start initiatives for green energy, and to preserve the dwindling reserves of fisheries around the island.

Luke wanted to help people. But he couldn't help much if he didn't have the money to do it.

To Jocelyn, Luke said, "Do you really want to know?"

She scowled. "Now you're being annoying again. Tell me if you want. I'm not going to beg for it."

Luke stepped closer, so close that he could see the specks of gold in her eyes.

"I have to get married within a year. Or I don't get my inheritance. Oh, and did I mention my dad was written out of my grandma's will? So it's all on me to save the family."

Jocelyn's eyes had progressively widened at each word. "Wow," was all she said finally.

"And I don't exactly have a bunch of women lined up to marry me."

"What about that ex-girlfriend of yours? Ginny Something?"

"Paying attention to who I'm dating? I'm surprised you'd care, sweetheart."

Jocelyn rolled her eyes. "It's a small town. I hear about your exploits even when I don't want to."

"Ginny is engaged already." Luke desperately wished he had another drink right then, admitting that fact. "She wanted to get married before I was ready. Besides, she only wanted me for my money."

Jocelyn wrinkled her nose. "Too bad she didn't wait around for you. She could've had her cake and eaten it, too."

Luke laughed, but it was a bitter laugh. "I need to find a woman to marry me so I can get money but who doesn't want to marry me for my money."

"Sounds like you're in a pickle." Jocelyn patted him on the shoulder.

The touch of her hand, the warmth of her fingers—those two things made his heart race. And yes, it made his cock harden, too.

He didn't know why he found Jocelyn Gray so attractive. She was a huge pain in the ass. She was a cat that swiped at you for no reason at all times. A normal, sensible person would want a cat that actually liked its owner.

Maybe if you got her out of your system, you could move on already, his brain whispered.

Jocelyn wouldn't marry a man just for a slice of his inheritance. Luke was confident in that fact. She had too much pride.

She'd probably only let him bandage her finger earlier because she'd been too woozy to protest. She was independent to the point of it being annoying.

"Maybe that woman does exist. One who would marry me just for me," Luke eventually mused aloud.

Jocelyn frowned. "But you said your ex is already with someone else."

He reached forward and brushed a silky piece of hair from her forehead.

"Not Ginny. You. How about it? Will you marry me, Jocelyn?"

CHAPTER FOUR

By the time a third diner sent back their plate because the burger had onions on it, Jocelyn was tempted to set the kitchen on fire. Mostly because she'd been the one making these basic mistakes.

Kelly, her sous chef, said in a voice that sounded meek but was anything but, "Do you want me to remake this?"

Jocelyn swallowed the retort on the tip of her tongue. "No. I can do it. Just let me finish this plate. Can you check on the salads?"

Jocelyn rarely made mistakes in the kitchen. Detail-oriented and anal, she hated when she screwed up an order. And she couldn't blame anyone but herself. The ticket read NO ONIONS in all caps. Clearly, her mind was floating miles above the earth instead of focusing on her job.

During a lull in the service, Gwen, Jocelyn's fellow co-owner and boss/friend, stepped into the kitchen. "Jocelyn, can we talk?"

Kelly smiled; the rest of the staff, though, made sure to

keep their reactions to themselves. At least until Jocelyn was out of sight.

"I heard there's been issues tonight with orders," said Gwen. The words were gentle, so gentle that Jocelyn wished they'd been an accusation.

"Yes. My fault entirely. I've already spoken with each of the diners and offered to comp their dinners."

Gwen frowned. "How many tonight?"

Jocelyn wanted to melt into the floor. "Three."

Gwen made a sound in her throat. She then gestured for Jocelyn to sit, which was really the last thing Jocelyn wanted to do. She wanted to return to her kitchen, her domain, and just cook until every thought bouncing around in her head melted away.

"Is something wrong? I've never seen you make this many mistakes in a night," said Gwen.

Luke Wright asked me to marry him two weeks ago. But not because he loves me. No, it's because he won't get his inheritance if he doesn't get married.

Because who would marry a harpy like Jocelyn for love? Although Jocelyn had been tempted to tell Luke to shove it, she'd also been impressed with his giant balls for even asking her.

"I'm fine," said Jocelyn. When Gwen looked skeptical, she added, "Really."

Jocelyn couldn't help but look at the diamond sparkling on Gwen's hand. Recently engaged with a man who was madly in love with her, Gwen had become more confident since opening the restaurant. She'd already opened and continued to run a successful bed and breakfast just next door. When she'd come to Jocelyn, asking for her help in realizing her dream of opening a restaurant, Jocelyn had jumped at the chance.

A green snake of jealousy coiled around Jocelyn's heart. Gwen was so kind, so lovable, that she deserved a man like Jack to adore her. But in the dark of the night, when Jocelyn felt the loneliest, she wondered if she'd ever be as lucky as Gwen.

"We're friends, aren't we?" said Gwen.

Jocelyn nodded.

"Then I hope you know that you can come to me if you need to. God knows you listened to me during the Jack saga."

Jocelyn was both touched and deeply uncomfortable. The thought of telling Gwen about Luke's marriage proposal would be humiliating. To admit that a man like Luke would only want Jocelyn so he could get a huge payout?

"I've just had a lot going on right now," hedged Jocelyn. "My family, mostly." *Not entirely a lie.*

"I've noticed that Luke has been coming around here a lot. But most nights he doesn't order any food. Maybe a drink or two, but that's it."

Jocelyn had also noticed. She'd told him that she'd think about his offer and give him an answer by the end of the month. The deadline was looming now, just two days away. And Luke, because he apparently loved to torment Jocelyn, had made a point to come to the restaurant nearly every evening since. Always alone, too.

"Luke does whatever he wants," said Jocelyn.

"You sure you haven't been distracted by him?" Gwen's eyebrows waggled.

"I never think about him." *Now you're really just lying through your teeth.*

"Okaaaaay." Gwen's lips curved into a smile. "You can go now."

Jocelyn let out a relieved breath. "Praise God."

THAT EVENING, Jocelyn had hoped to have a quiet night with her dad and Fluffer, but apparently the universe was not going to let that happen.

Her younger sister Alex was at the house when Jocelyn came in. Five years younger than Jocelyn, Alex was outgoing and had a penchant for getting into trouble. It didn't help that she was a pretty girl, with her dark chestnut hair and sparkling eyes. Compared to Alex, Jocelyn had always seemed pale and drab. More than once, she'd been asked why she couldn't be more fun like her little sister.

Jocelyn loved her sister. She did, but they'd never seen eye to eye on much of anything. When Jocelyn said *right*, Alex would say *left* just to be frustrating. When Alex had come home one day to announce that she'd purchased the lone bookstore on Hazel Island despite the fact that the business had been in the red for years, Jocelyn had gotten into a blowout fight with her.

Alex had needed a steady income. Not just for herself, but to help their dad. But she'd blown the little savings she had to buy the place despite Jocelyn telling her not to.

Alex was currently feeding Fluffer slices of apple, a food that the rabbit should only have very occasionally. "Joss! Look, he loves apples so much," said Alex with a smile.

Fluffer just kept chowing down without so much as a glance at his owner.

"Did he eat his regular dinner first?" said Jocelyn.

Alex shrugged. "Not sure. I just wanted to give him something he'd like."

Jocelyn had to bite her tongue to keep from snapping. It was only their dad's glance toward Jocelyn that made her swallow her retort.

"Are you staying for dinner, Alex?" said Jocelyn finally.

"Of course. Why else would I come over?" She scrunched up her nose at their dad, making him laugh.

Alex was good at that, making people laugh. Jocelyn had never been able to be that person. Lively, the center of attention. Then again, Jocelyn had always preferred to stay out of the spotlight, unless it was for her cooking.

The evening ended up being pleasant. Alex entertained their dad with stories of ridiculous customers coming into the bookstore.

"This guy seriously wanted to order an entire set of print encyclopedias and was mad we couldn't get the order in by tomorrow," said Alex as she rolled her eyes. "Who wants encyclopedias nowadays? Just Google it!"

"Once upon a time, there was no such thing as Google," said Pete sagely.

"Well, yeah. But this isn't 1965."

"You wouldn't last a day without your phone in your hand." Despite the remark, Pete smiled.

Alex just shrugged a shoulder. "Probably not. But why should I?" As she said the words, she was scrolling on her phone.

"Can you help with dishes?" said Jocelyn from the kitchen to her sister.

"One sec."

Jocelyn's annoyance grew when Alex's "one second" turned into five minutes, then ten. In a bad mood again, Jocelyn finished the dishes without another word.

"Did you wash all of the dishes?" was Alex's question when Jocelyn returned to the living room. "I said I'd help."

"It's fine," said Jocelyn tersely.

"Sorry, I got distracted. There's this thing with the bookstore, it's been my entire focus and I just totally forgot I'd said I'd help—"

"It's fine." Jocelyn's jaw hurt from grinding her teeth.

She knew she was being a bitch. Alex usually helped with the dishes, and she could generally be counted on to help with other chores if asked.

Jocelyn forced herself to take a deep breath, even as she saw from her peripheral vision Alex rolling her eyes. She talked to their dad instead and played with Fluffer, making all of them laugh at his antics.

But the good mood vanished when Alex held up some envelopes she'd found on the counter right as she was about to leave. "Dad, what are these?" she said.

Pete stiffened. Jocelyn raised an eyebrow. Going over to Alex, she took the envelopes. One had been opened, but not the other two.

They were from the bank. As Jocelyn read the documents inside the first envelope, her blood ran cold. She handed them to Alex without a word.

Alex paled. When she opened her mouth to call for their

dad, Jocelyn shushed her and took her to her room to talk in private.

"You don't have to drag me," muttered Alex as Jocelyn shut the door. "And besides, Dad opened that first one himself."

Jocelyn felt like the walls were closing in on her. She'd known their dad's medical bills were piling up. But she hadn't known until recently that he hadn't been paying the mortgage. Apparently, he'd missed multiple payments. Now the bank was threatening foreclosure.

Alex sat down next to Jocelyn. "What do we do?" she said finally.

"We help Dad as much as we can." Jocelyn sighed. A headache began to pulse in her temples. "If he loses the house, he'll probably have to go into a nursing home."

"He can come live with me. We can't dump him in some home."

"In your studio apartment? Besides, we both know a two-bedroom apartment on the island would cost more in rent than the mortgage."

Alex didn't have an answer to that. Jocelyn's mind was whirling, thinking of ways to make more money, to get the bank from following through on foreclosure.

But she had very little savings. She lived paycheck to paycheck. Sure, she could find another job, but the island was small. It was unlikely she'd find something that paid better than she was already making as a chef.

"How much do you have in savings?" said Jocelyn. "I only have a thousand, I think."

Alex wasn't looking at Jocelyn. Instead, she was staring at her feet. That made Jocelyn sit up straight.

"The bookstore…" Alex swallowed audibly. "It's not doing great lately."

"Define 'not great.'"

"I'm in the red."

Jocelyn felt sick. "How much in debt are you?"

"I don't know." Alex's voice was a whisper.

"Ballpark estimate."

A moment passed, then finally, Alex replied, "Hundred grand, give or take."

"One hundred thousand dollars!" Jocelyn nearly screeched the number. "I thought you'd say a fraction of that. Something manageable. Alexandra, how did you get that deep into debt?"

"I don't know! I was just hoping things would turn around, and then it kept getting worse and worse. I think I kept digging a hole to get out of the other hole I'd already dug."

"So you have nothing. I have nothing. Dad has nothing."

Just imagining putting their dad in a nursing home made Jocelyn want to cry. He'd always taken care of them, but now… Now his two daughters couldn't help him. He'd die in some home, and it'd be Jocelyn's fault.

"Why did you buy that stupid bookstore?" said Jocelyn savagely. "I told you not to do it. That it was a money-sink."

"It wasn't at first!"

"For the first year, you buying it made it a novelty again. After that, everybody returned to reading eBooks, like I told you they would."

Jocelyn knew she was being cruel, that her sister wasn't

the reason they were in this mess. Not really, but Alex's money troubles certainly didn't help, either.

"It's not your problem. It's mine." Alex stood up. "I don't need some lecture from you. You always treat me like a child."

"Because you keep acting like one! You can't keep being impulsive and think everything will just work out. I'm not going to keep saving your ass because you jump before you look."

"I never once asked you to save me. That was *you*. You intervene and think you're helping, but you just make things worse." Now there were tears in Alex's eyes. "I'll find the money to help Dad as best as I can. It's not just on you. But the bookstore? It's not your issue to solve."

When Alex left with only a brief goodbye and kiss for their dad, Jocelyn waited for their dad to question her. But when he didn't and merely stared blindly at the TV, Jocelyn knew he was fighting his own anxiety.

"It's bad, isn't it, Joss?" said Pete in a low voice before they went to bed.

"We'll figure it out." She hugged her dad. "We always do."

He hugged her tightly. "If anyone can figure things out, it's you. You've always been a smart girl. And strong. So strong."

Jocelyn wished sometimes she didn't have to keep being strong. She'd had to be strong for her family ever since their mom had left in the middle of the night without a word.

Jocelyn had been ten; Alex, five. Pete had worked full-time, so the responsibility of mothering had fallen on Jocelyn.

She was the one who'd made sure Alex had her lunch before she got on the bus for school. She was the one who made them dinner, who made sure Alex had clean clothes and made sure she took a bath, even when she'd protested.

"You'll need to look out for your little sister," their dad had told Jocelyn as they'd grown. "I'll do my best, but I have to keep a roof over our head."

And he had. He'd worked twelve-hour days for years. Sometimes he'd take a late shift, and Jocelyn would go into his bedroom in the morning before school to give him a kiss. He'd be sleepy, but he'd always return the gesture.

But Alex, as she'd gotten older—she hadn't appreciated Jocelyn mothering her. She'd balked when Jocelyn had instituted a curfew when she'd turned thirteen. When Jocelyn had gotten wind that Alex was dating an older boy, Jocelyn had grounded her sister when she'd tried to sneak out to see him one night.

Although their dad had tried to be a parent, he simply hadn't been around enough to do so. It had fallen on Jocelyn.

And Jocelyn had known that she had to keep things in order, that she had to keep her sister on a tight leash, otherwise the fragile house of cards she'd built would come tumbling down.

If Jocelyn tried to control every aspect of her own life because she felt so out of control inwardly, she kept that thought to herself. Even when teenage Alex told her she hated her. That she'd ruined her life. Jocelyn had carried on, because what choice did she have?

Now, though, maybe she could make things easier. All she had to do was marry a man she loathed.

CHAPTER FIVE

The Wright mansion never failed to make Luke feel lonely. Despite the staff and his own parents residing there, the house was so large that it was easy to avoid any human contact if you wanted to.

Luke had never liked living in the place. Sure, it had amazing views of the ocean and mountains, and he certainly couldn't complain about living in such a nice house. But when he'd gone to friends' houses, he'd always been reminded of how strange his own family was by comparison.

And then Tristan had run off and things had never been the same.

Luke knocked on his mom's door, hearing dogs barking before he heard his mom telling him he could enter. Juliet Wright's bedroom was separate from her husband's, as it had been for the past twenty years. The furniture and bedding were all in various shades of black, white, and gray. Juliet hated color and seemed to prefer to live her life solely in black and white.

Even her dogs were her preferred colors. When once Gregory had given her a brown Pomeranian, she'd returned the dog for a white one a week later.

At the moment, she was lounging on a settee like some princess in a fairy tale. She was feeding bites of cheese to Cosmo. Another dog named Teddy was snoring on a velvet cushion nearby.

"Mom," said Luke as he bent down to kiss her cheek.

Cosmo growled when Luke got too close, but Luke just ignored him. He'd learned long ago that his mom's dogs were mostly bark and very lazy bite.

"Cosmo has learned a new trick. He just did it this morning." Juliet raised another bite of cheese high up and said in a sickly sweet voice, "Play dead. No, play dead. Oh, bad dog. No cheese for you, then."

Cosmo did not like this. He whined, getting louder and louder, until Juliet finally relented and fed him that last cube of cheese.

Luke couldn't say this mom had been the most amazing mother ever. She'd often been busy playing society wife, and she didn't exactly enjoy making cookies and driving her kids to soccer practice. But she'd always made birthdays and other holidays special, and she'd done her best to keep her boys happy. When Tristan had had his falling-out with their parents, Luke knew that his mom had been devastated when Tristan had cut contact.

And if Luke didn't marry and receive his inheritance, his mom would struggle. His gut twisted at the thought. Yes, she didn't need to live in a mansion. She didn't need to feed her Pomeranians expensive cheese.

But Luke had grown up with the idea that he'd lead the

family when his dad passed. What kind of a son would he be if he abandoned either parent in their time of need?

Juliet sat up and pointed at a pad of paper on the coffee table. "I made you a list of possible wives. Don't make a face, now. They're all eligible and would make any man a good wife."

Luke's lips twisted. "You sound like a Jane Austen novel."

"Who? You know I don't like to read." She cooed at Teddy, who'd yawned and waddled over for some pats.

Luke glanced over the list, grimacing as he read. He'd met most of these women. They *were* eligible: rich, beautiful, and educated. He'd even dated a few of them.

But they all wanted money and prestige more than they wanted love. A marriage with any of them would be merely an arrangement to benefit them both. Would they even sleep together? Luke figured they would, until they had children, and then they'd have separate bedrooms like his own parents.

As Luke thought of marriage, he thought of his impulsive proposal to Jocelyn. He'd been shocked she hadn't cut his dick off when he'd said the words. She'd been so shocked she'd said *nothing*.

"What about marrying for love?" said Luke suddenly.

Juliet glanced at him. "Oh, sweetheart. I didn't know you were such a romantic. But love may come. If not, that's what mistresses are for."

"Is that what Dad has done?"

His mom barely reacted. "Oh, probably. I don't ask, and he doesn't say. It works quite well for us both."

Luke felt his stomach turn. "What about you?"

Juliet picked up Cosmo. "A lady never tells."

Luke just grimaced again and forced himself to stop thinking about his parents having affairs. Maybe he was naive to think he could find a woman who'd want to marry him for him alone.

Jocelyn didn't jump at your proposal…

She might not have jumped at it, but considering how fast she'd gotten him out of the restaurant, she had no interest in saying yes.

"Maybe I can find a woman, fall in love, and marry her within a year," said Luke.

"You could. But what happens when she finds out you need to marry?" Juliet stroked Cosmo behind his ears.

"I'd tell her from the beginning."

Juliet said nothing.

Luke knew he was being ridiculous. If he were honest from the get-go, he'd risk a woman saying yes solely for the money. If he didn't mention the money, what happened when he received his inheritance? Would she accept that he'd just left out that little detail?

Luke sighed. "I'll find someone," he said as he stood up. "Don't worry. I'll make sure you're taken care of."

Juliet squeezed his hand. "I know. You're a good son."

Luke wished he felt the same. At the moment, he was tempted to shirk his responsibilities and run off to some uninhabited island.

He also wished he could talk to his brother. Luke had tried to find out where Tristan was living and a phone number, but he'd never had any luck. His brother apparently did not want his family to find him.

But the lawyer needed to get in contact with Tristan so

he could receive his part of the inheritance. A portion, Luke knew, that wouldn't be nearly enough to help their parents.

Not that Tristan would give them a dime. Luke doubted his brother had changed in that regard.

In his office, Luke began making calls. Hiring a private investigator to find his prodigal brother felt like overkill, but Luke was desperate. And desperate times called for desperate measures.

LUKE AWOKE to someone shaking his shoulder. Maggie, the Wrights' housekeeper, was looming over him. "Sir, there's someone downstairs to see you."

Luke rubbed his eyes. His bedroom was still dim; the sun hadn't even risen yet. "Is it an emergency? Is someone bleeding?"

"No blood, but she insisted."

Any sleepiness he felt disappeared in that moment. "She" could only mean one person. "Show her to my office."

After quickly dressing, he hurried to his office, his heart pounding in anticipation. He wasn't sure if he was more excited about Jocelyn telling him yes or telling him to go to hell.

Jocelyn was standing in front of his desk, her arms crossed. She had her hair down, which was unusual for her. Luke had to admit he couldn't remember the last time he'd seen her without her hair in a tight bun or ponytail. She had beautiful hair, pale blond and silky, falling in soft waves to below her shoulders.

Luke made a point to sit in his office chair, putting his feet up on his desk. He gestured for Jocelyn to sit. "Do you know what time it is?" he said amiably.

Jocelyn didn't sit. "I have to get to work early today." Her lips lifted into a smirk. "Were you still sleeping?"

"At six in the morning? Yes, Jocelyn, I was sleeping. Most people are doing the same."

"Only people who don't have to get up and work."

So, that was how this was going to go? Luke should've downed a few cups of coffee to steel himself before meeting Jocelyn. As it were, he'd have to make some himself right here.

"Do you want coffee? I'm not nearly awake enough for this conversation." He went to the coffee pot in the corner. He'd never actually used the device before. It was one of those machines that used those funny pod things.

Luke searched for the pods, coming up short, when he heard Jocelyn come up behind him. "Need any help?" she said sweetly. Too sweetly, he thought.

"I don't know where Maggie put the pods." He opened another cabinet and found a box. "Here we go. Wait, is there water in this thing?"

Jocelyn chuckled and finally took over making coffee. She filled the reservoir with water and placed two pods in the machine. It started making noise a few moments later.

"I could've figured it out," muttered Luke.

"I didn't want to wait an hour for you to realize you just needed to read the directions." Jocelyn pointed to the manual that was behind the machine.

Luke growled. "How did you survive without someone strangling you?"

"I think that would be considered murder. Which is illegal." Jocelyn raised her eyebrows. "We've had this discussion before. Although I think I was the one who wanted to murder you."

"One thing we have in common: the desire to strangle each other."

By the time they both had their mugs of coffee, Luke's mood had soured. Even the taste of hot coffee wasn't enough.

It didn't help that he was remembering with painful clarity that afternoon when he'd held Jocelyn in his arms in this very room. How soft she'd felt, how her eyes had widened and how the furrow in her forehead had disappeared. She'd *surrendered* to him. If he hadn't felt it himself, he'd never have believed she was capable of it.

But Jocelyn wasn't surrendering to him now. She'd sat down across from him reluctantly, her back straight as an arrow. Her blouse was buttoned-up to her chin; her slacks were baggy and hid her shape. Clearly, she hadn't come here to seduce him.

"I wanted to give you my answer," said Jocelyn finally. She cleared her throat. "It's a yes."

Luke nearly choked on his coffee. Coughing, he took another drink. But that just burned his throat. *This is going as badly as I would've expected*, he thought irritably.

He leaned toward Jocelyn, his gaze intent on her face. "Yes? Tell me what you're saying yes to."

"You know what I'm talking about."

"I want you to say it."

A blush climbed up her cheeks. But she didn't break eye

contact, even as she fidgeted with her hands. "I'll marry you," she ground out.

He couldn't help but bark out a laugh. "You sound like you're agreeing to be tortured."

"Aren't I?"

That made him snort. "So dramatic, Jocelyn. Any woman would love to be in your position."

"Then why haven't you found one of those women? If they're so plentiful?"

Luke had no answer to that. If he were honest, he'd barely looked. Perhaps in the back of his mind, he'd hoped this entire situation would simply resolve itself. That Grammy had just been playing a terrible joke on them all and would reappear one day to yell, YOU'VE BEEN PUNKED.

But he knew there was no punking. Ashton Kutcher was not going to appear around the corner, either. This was all too real.

And now Jocelyn Gray was saying yes to marrying him.

Rising, Luke went to stand in front of Jocelyn, peering down at her. He watched as she glanced away, how she was picking at a thread on her pants. Her cheeks kept getting redder. That fact alone brought him pleasure.

"You'll marry me," he said.

She raised her chin. "Yes."

"You'll live with me."

"Obviously."

"You'll vow to honor and cherish me. Till death do us part." He loomed over her now. "You'll be my dutiful, obedient little wife."

"Obedient? You've got to be kidding."

"Yes, obedient." He breathed the words next to the shell of her ear. "You'll do as I tell you. I have the upper hand, you see. You're not the only woman in the world. I could choose anyone. So if you want to marry me, you'll play the part of a loving wife."

Her breathing had quickened. Even with her buttoned-up blouse, he could see her nipples hardening against the fabric.

"You'll share my bed," he continued, the words alone sending flames through his body. "And I'll have you whenever I want."

That made her try to stand up, but Luke looming over her prevented her from getting up.

"I'm not having sex with you," she shot back.

He grinned. "Are you saying we're going to have a platonic marriage?"

"It's not going to be a real marriage anyway. We're doing this so you get your inheritance."

That reminder made Luke resume leaning against his desk. Crossing his arms, he cocked an eyebrow.

"Why are you saying yes? Is it for my money?" he said. The words came out harsh, and he saw Jocelyn flinch.

"I don't want your money."

"I don't believe you."

Her eyes flashed. "Believe what you want."

Luke considered her. He knew she wasn't doing this out of the goodness of her heart. And she certainly wasn't doing it because she cared about him. For all he knew, she was agreeing simply to fuck with his head.

"I'll draw up a contract," he said. "We'll go over it before we have the ceremony."

"What kind of contract?" She wrinkled her nose. "Is this some kind of sex dungeon scenario? Please tell me you don't have a red room."

That made him laugh. "You wish, sweetheart. No, I'm not talking about a sex contract." But at the mention of it, he tapped his chin. "Then again, that might be a good idea. I will have needs, you know. If I'm to be a loyal husband, that is."

"You're disgusting." Jocelyn stood up and grabbed her bag. "I'm not listening to this."

"Oh, so you're reneging on our deal?"

That stopped her. He could see her struggling. She wanted to throw her bag in his face, but her logical brain was telling her to swallow her rage.

He had to admit, cornering Jocelyn was insanely amusing to him. And to have her do what he wanted, and she had to comply…

Absolutely delicious.

"No," she finally said in a low voice. "I'm still in this."

"Good." Luke rounded on her and, before she could react, wrapped an arm around her waist. "Let's seal the deal."

Her eyes widened. Before she could protest, he kissed her.

She resisted, but only for a moment. Then she melted, and then her hands were clutching at his shirt.

She tasted of coffee, her mouth silky-sweet. Luke couldn't help but run his fingers through her hair, pressing her against him until he could feel all of her curves. His cock hardened just from this simple kiss.

He broke the embrace. "That was good. But you should use more tongue."

Jocelyn reared back. She hissed at him like an enraged cat, which just made him laugh.

"I love seeing you angry," he said, still laughing. "It's sexy as fuck."

"Go to hell," she snapped.

"Only with you in tow." Smiling, he added, "So I'll talk to you soon?"

Jocelyn just sighed in despair.

CHAPTER SIX

For days, Jocelyn would have to remind herself that she'd agreed to marry Luke Wright. That he was drawing up a marriage contract right that moment.

She'd pinch herself, convinced she was dreaming, but then real life intruded. And inevitably, Luke would text her with questions:

When is your birthday?

What are you parents' names?

Where were you born?

Among other personal questions. She half-expected him to ask for her to go to a doctor for a physical so he could view the results. Maybe even do the physical himself just to be safe.

The following Friday, when the restaurant was slow in the morning, Jocelyn returned to the Wright mansion to hash out the contract. When she arrived, Maggie told her with pursed lips that Mr. Luke was busy but would be down in a few minutes.

"We agreed I'd come here at eight," said Jocelyn.

"It's only seven-fifty, ma'am." Maggie seemed to find Jocelyn's early arrival offensive. "You may wait in the parlor. Can I get you anything to drink?"

Jocelyn declined a beverage, not entirely certain Maggie wouldn't find a way to spike it with something. The house-keeper seemed especially protective of the family.

Did she know why Jocelyn was here? Jocelyn grimaced. No matter what story she and Luke came up with, she had a feeling few people would believe they'd suddenly fallen madly in love.

Jocelyn found that she couldn't just sit and stare at her phone. Wandering, she took in the parlor, which was deco-rated in shades of blue. Blue wallpaper, blue curtains, blue furniture. Despite the monochromatic theme, it was a beau-tiful room that was filled with tons of natural light from bay windows that faced east. There was a fireplace on one side. Other side tables and dressers were covered in family photos.

Jocelyn gazed at the photos. One photo was of a family of four, the older boy obviously Luke. The younger boy must be his younger brother, Tristan. Jocelyn had seen Tristan in school, but beyond that, she had no idea why he'd seemingly disappeared from Hazel Island. Considering there were no photos of Tristan as an adult, Jocelyn had a feeling that was a mystery the family wasn't interested in talking about.

There were more photos of Luke growing up: fishing, sailing, and opening Christmas presents. One photo was of him and an older woman. His grandmother? Jocelyn picked up the framed photo and smiled. The woman had mischief in her eyes despite the formal smile on her face. She was holding Luke in her arms, but he was focused on opening whatever gift she'd probably just given him. He looked maybe seven years old.

Jocelyn realized that the painting on the wall above the photos was of this grandmother. The one who'd made the provision that Luke had to marry to receive his inheritance.

In the painting, she was much younger, probably around Jocelyn's age now. She was beautiful, with dark brown hair curled and bobbed in the fashion of the day. Her lips were curled in a smile similar to the one in the later photo.

"That's Granny," said Luke's voice behind Jocelyn's shoulder.

Jocelyn started. She hadn't even heard him enter the room.

"Good lord, you nearly gave me a heart attack," she said.

"We wouldn't want you to die. At least not until you've signed on the dotted line first."

Jocelyn rolled her eyes. She gestured toward the painting. "She's the one who wants you to get married so badly?"

Luke's smile faded as he gazed at the portrait. "Granny was a force to be reckoned with. She was always kind to me, but she essentially ran the family her entire life. When she married my grandfather, he changed his last name to Wright."

"Really? I'm sure that raised a lot of eyebrows at the time."

"Oh, his family was pissed. They pretty much disowned him, but Grandpa adored Granny. He was the great love of her life." Luke's eyes turned sad. "I never knew him. He died before I was born, but Granny told me stories about them often."

Jocelyn looked at the face in the portrait with new appreciation. "Although I can't say I approve of her tactics, I wish I could've met her. She sounds fascinating."

"She was. You would've liked her. She would've said you had gumption."

That made Jocelyn smile. For a moment, she and Luke smiled at each other, the moment stretching in its intimacy. She felt her heart start pounding again. This time, it wasn't from being surprised. It was being so close to Luke.

He broke the moment when he said, "We should get to work."

After that, Luke was focused solely on the contract and their marriage. Where they would live, what they would tell people, how much Jocelyn would receive as an allowance, and so many other things that Jocelyn's head was spinning within twenty minutes.

"An allowance?" She wrinkled her nose at the word. "Am I ten years old?"

"As my wife, you'll be entitled to certain benefits. One of those is money." Luke raised an eyebrow. "Are you turning down money, dearest fiancée?"

Jocelyn swallowed hard. She wanted to throw the offer in his face, but she needed money. Just yesterday, her dad had gotten another notice in the mail that payment for one of his medical bills was overdue. Way overdue. If the balance wasn't paid by the end of the month, it'd go straight to collections.

"No, I'm not turning down money," she replied in a tight voice.

"Good. We can negotiate the exact amount later. But don't expect anything extravagant. I won't have access to my inheritance before a year is up."

Jocelyn felt a chill drip down her spine. "A year?"

"Yeah, a year. At the very least." He stared at her. "I told you that, didn't I?"

She couldn't remember. She'd been so focused on the possibility of finding a way to help her dad in a substantial way that she hadn't considered how long she'd be on the hook.

Married to Luke and living with him for a year? That thought alone made her want to get up and run far, far away.

Is it because you have no self-control around him? her mind whispered slyly.

Considering she'd let him kiss her during their last meeting, her self-control barely existed around Luke Wright. If she weren't careful, she'd fall for him, and then what?

It wasn't like he'd want to stay married to her. She'd end up broken-hearted and hating herself for being a complete idiot.

"No, I mean, you probably did. It just hit me how long a year is," said Jocelyn.

"Three hundred and sixty-five days, to be exact." He glanced at his phone. "Wait, add another day. Next year is a leap year."

Jocelyn just groaned as he chuckled.

They continued negotiations throughout the morning. Despite her initial trepidation, Jocelyn found herself almost enjoying herself. She hated to admit it, but Luke was being fair with her. Although she was suspicious he'd still screw her over, he'd yet to do anything shady.

It was annoying. Most of all, it made her want to like him.

"We need to come up with a story people will believe as to why we got married so quickly," said Luke two hours into their meeting.

"Who all knows about this scheme?"

"My parents, Granny's lawyer. Granny's friend, Opal. And us. That's it."

Jocelyn imagined telling her dad and hated that she'd have to lie to him. And Alex! Would Alex buy any story they came up with?

"My sister is going to lose her mind," muttered Jocelyn.

"Ah yes. She's a spitfire."

Luke sounded like he admired that trait in Alex, which made jealousy prick Jocelyn's heart.

Don't be stupid. Besides, this is all business. This isn't about feelings.

At the thought of her dad, Jocelyn's jealousy turned instantly to guilt. How could she be talking about moving in with Luke without mentioning her dad? He couldn't live on his own. It was why she'd returned to Hazel Island in the first place.

Clearly her head was in the clouds. Staying focused was apparently impossible when Luke was involved. Jocelyn knew that didn't bode well for her at all.

"What's that face?" said Luke.

"Am I making a face?"

"You look like you just swallowed a bug."

"I mean, I always make that face when I'm with you." But she smiled when she said the words.

"Jocelyn Gray, did you just make a *joke?*" Luke put a hand to his chest. "I didn't know you could."

"I'm hilarious when you aren't around."

"Huh." His expression turned serious. "But why the face?"

"My dad. I can't believe I didn't bring this up before."

She felt a blush creeping up her face. She was mortified at how selfishly she'd been thinking. Yes, she needed the money to help her dad, but she hadn't considered if Luke would want his brand-new father-in-law around.

"Your dad," Luke prodded.

"I don't know if you know this, but he's not in the greatest of health. He's had two strokes, one in the last three years. He can't live on his own. I mean, he'll tell you he can, but don't believe him."

"That's why you came back to the island?" Luke considered her. "I wondered why."

She blinked in surprise. Luke had wondered about her? Stupidly, she felt pleasure at the discovery. He'd thought about her beyond wishing her to fall to her doom from one of the many cliffs on Hazel Island.

"If we move in together, my dad would have to come with us." Jocelyn steeled herself. "I won't put him in a nursing home. He'd hate it. He wouldn't last long. Not that all homes are bad, but just the thought of moving him to one…" She fought back tears.

"You'd feel like you'd be abandoning him," said Luke softly. He handed her a tissue.

She dabbed at her eyes. "I don't know why I'm crying."

"You love your dad. It makes sense."

Jocelyn sniffled. The thought of leaving her dad in a home broke her heart. Worst of all, there weren't any homes here on the island. She'd have to send him somewhere else in the state. The closest large town was an hour-long ferry ride away. She had no idea what kinds of facilities it could offer.

She couldn't afford a nice place, anyway. Her dad would be at the mercy of whatever was available.

"Anyway," said Jocelyn, balling up the tissue in her fist, "I should've brought this up earlier. If you aren't okay with my dad living with us, I understand."

Luke considered her. Jocelyn waited for the ax to fall. If he said the deal was off, well, she couldn't blame him. It was one thing to agree to marry her; it was another to add her dad to the equation.

"Are you trying to get out of this?" said Luke.

Jocelyn stared. "What? No."

"Because it sounds like you're trying to get me to back out of it."

"I'm just saying you can back out if you want to. No hard feelings."

"Hmm. That's a statement I sincerely doubt." He shuffled some papers, then added, "I'm not going to force you to abandon your dad. We can work something out. If he'd rather not live with us, perhaps we can pay for a place next door. Or does he need care round the clock?"

The worry that had been pressing down on Jocelyn's heart lifted. "No, but he needs help with cleaning, cooking, sometimes with bathing. His mind is still intact, for the most part. He does tend to talk about the same five subjects, though."

"To be fair, doesn't everyone?" Luke raised a finger. "Weather, family, money, weather again, and their health. Did I miss anything?"

"I'm pretty sure people around here talk about the weather even more than that."

They smiled at each other, like they had down in the parlor. The connection Jocelyn had felt earlier buzzed with electricity. She suddenly had the wish that he'd kiss her again.

He seemed to read her mind because his nostrils flared. "We never talked about sex," he said roughly.

Jocelyn's traitorous heart fluttered. "Um, did we need to?"

Luke moved so he sat next to her on the sofa. His arm behind her head, he made her want to snuggle into his side. She could smell him now, a woodsy cologne that reminded her of the dense forests just outside. His eyes gleamed as he gazed down at her.

She licked her lips. His gaze darted to the subtle movement.

"Yeah, we need to talk about sex," he said. He didn't touch her as he added, "If we're going to make people believe we've fallen for each other, we can't act like touching each other makes us want to hurl."

Jocelyn fought back a laugh. "You want to hurl when you touch me?"

"The opposite. I have to fight not to touch you." He belied his own words when he traced the line of her jaw.

"Every atom of my being wants to throw you over my shoulder and fuck you senseless."

Jocelyn was blushing to her hairline. Her heart pounded, while blood pounded lower in her body as well.

"How caveman of you," she breathed. "I thought you were a gentleman."

He smiled wickedly. "The dirty fantasies I've had of you. You have no idea."

They were both breathing hard now. Jocelyn waited for him to kiss her again, waited for his mouth to move against her own.

But he stood up instead. Jocelyn was glad she was sitting down because she felt a little weak in the knees.

"We don't have to sleep together," said Luke, all business now. "But when we're in public, we'll need to be touchy-feely." His gaze fastened on her. "Can you do that? And act like you want it?"

Jocelyn bristled. "I'm not a fan of PDA."

"I'm not saying we'll need to make out in the middle of the street. But holding hands, brief kisses, hugs—you can do that with a smile?"

He said the words as a challenge, like he didn't believe she could do it. And damn him, it worked. Jocelyn hated when anyone doubted her own abilities.

She stood, mostly so he was no longer looming over her. "I'll be the most affectionate wife ever. You'll have to beg me to stop, I'll be so handsy."

Luke's lips twitched. "I'd pay money to see that."

She fluttered her eyelashes. Then she ran her fingers down his arm until she intertwined them with his own. Stepping closer until there was only a breath of space between their bodies, she whispered, "Are you nervous, dearest fiancé?"

His jaw clenched. "Why should I be?"

She reached their joined hands up, placing his right below her breast. If he moved even an inch, he'd cup the weight in his palm.

"You just seem out of sorts. That's all," she said. Her lips nearly touched his as she said the words.

"You're playing with fire," he growled.

"Oh, don't worry. I know how to deal with a fire. I'm a chef, after all."

Luke laughed. "Another joke. I think I'm in the Twilight Zone." Even as he said the words, he cupped the back of her neck, his touch making her shiver.

"What are we doing?" Jocelyn blurted the words as the moment lengthened painfully.

Luke just shook his head. "Fuck me if I know."

Jocelyn hadn't always disliked Luke Wright. In fact, she'd been in love with him many years ago.

The Grays and the Wrights, despite both living on the same small island, didn't really run in the same circles. Growing up, Jocelyn had watched the Wright boys from afar, as most people did who weren't invited to the illustrious Wright mansion.

Luke had been in Jocelyn's class, while Tristan had been a few grades below her. Luke had been handsome, charming, and popular. He'd played lacrosse, run track, and been crowned both homecoming king and prom king. He'd lived a charmed life, as far as Jocelyn could tell.

He always wore brand-new designer clothes to school. Although most of the islanders were solidly middle class, Jocelyn and Alex had been the select few that people would whisper about being poor.

I heard they get free breakfasts, Jocelyn would hear more than once growing up. *I heard they only buy from the thrift shop*, was another one.

Jocelyn hadn't cared about the whispers, but Alex had. Alex had always wanted to fit in. She'd begged Jocelyn more than once to let her spend some exorbitant amount of money on a handbag or a pair of jeans. It got to a point that Alex went behind Jocelyn's back to get a job to earn her own money. Although Jocelyn had been annoyed, she'd been grudgingly impressed at her younger sister's drive.

When Jocelyn had been seventeen and a senior in high school, she'd ended up in the same PE class as Luke Wright of all people. A PE class that had had all of ten students, because it was at an awkward time. Most students preferred to sweat either first thing in the morning or right before they could go home.

Luke charmed the teacher right off the bat. Jocelyn watched him with interest. She was usually the quiet kid in the back who preferred not to be noticed. She had her own small group of friends, but nothing like Luke had. He somehow made friends with everyone.

One day, they were starting a week of doing yoga. Their teacher, Ms. Tyson, liked to try all different kinds of activities. The week before they'd spent their time working out to cheesy aerobics videos straight from 1985.

Jocelyn was surprised when Luke put his mat down next to her. He'd been late, so he hadn't gotten his usual spot near the front. He shot Jocelyn a smile before going into downward dog pose.

Jocelyn blushed. She knew his smiling at her meant nothing. Luke smiled at everybody: the teachers, pretty girls, even the janitors. It was as if he needed everyone within a one-mile radius to like him. Jocelyn found it rather strange. It seemed a lot of effort for little payoff.

"Hey," whispered Luke when they stood up to do tree pose. "You're in my Spanish class, right? Is there a quiz today?"

Jocelyn nodded. "On the subjunctive."

Luke cursed. "I thought it wasn't until Friday. Crap. Can I borrow your notes?"

Ms. Tyson shot them both a look that said to be quiet and listen to the meditative music instead. Jocelyn was rather tempted to tell Luke to shove it, but he'd asked nicely enough. Sighing inwardly, she replied quietly, "Meet me after class."

She handed over her notes outside the locker rooms. "Won't you need them?" said Luke.

"I studied last night. I'm good."

As luck would have it, their Spanish teacher was out sick and the quiz was, in fact, postponed until Monday. But Luke didn't return Jocelyn's notes until Friday, when he found her near the cafeteria eating lunch. Her two good friends didn't have the same lunch period as Jocelyn, so she happened to be alone right then.

"Hey, thanks a lot," said Luke, handing the notes over. "You have really nice handwriting, by the way."

Jocelyn blushed. "Thanks," she muttered into her sandwich. She waited for Luke to leave, but he ended up sitting down next to her. She looked at him with confusion.

"What are you doing?" she finally blurted after he'd taken a few bites of his own sandwich.

"Eating."

"Obviously. I meant, why are you sitting with me?"

Luke shrugged. "I thought I'd try something different today."

Jocelyn narrowed her eyes in suspicion. She wondered if this was a bizarre prank. Even as students walked past them and whispered to each other, Luke didn't seem to notice the attention. He was intent on eating.

Like most teenage boys, he seemed to inhale anything edible with superhuman speed. Jocelyn didn't know how he managed to pack away that much food. Despite the amount, he was relatively thin, although he'd gotten more muscular within the last year. Jocelyn was abashed that she'd noticed.

"There's one thing about the subjunctive I don't get," said Luke suddenly.

Jocelyn waited, popping another grape into her mouth.

"Do I use it here? Because that's not a thing in English, so it always confuses me."

Jocelyn explained the concept, feeling her confidence grow as Luke seemed to understand what she meant. She might not feel comfortable eating lunch with a guy like him, but she'd always feel comfortable showing how much she knew.

"You know, we should form a study group. My Spanish grade has always been my worst," said Luke.

Despite her reservations, Jocelyn found herself agreeing. She told herself it wasn't because she wanted to spend more time with Luke. She was going to help him with his Spanish, and she'd get in more study time. It was a win-win situation.

But Jocelyn was surprised upon arriving to their first study session that there was no group. It was just Jocelyn and Luke sitting at a local coffee place. Even worse, Luke chose a spot that felt painfully intimate, like they were the only two people in existence.

As the days passed, their study sessions became less about Spanish and more about getting to know one another. Luke complained about his parents' high expectations, about how his dad had threatened to pull him out of lacrosse if he didn't graduate with a 4.0 GPA.

"I already have a scholarship to the University of Washington, plus offers from Oregon State and even UCLA," he said as he flicked a straw wrapper across the table. "What does it matter? As long as I don't flunk any classes, who cares?"

Jocelyn, though, just rolled her eyes at him. At Luke's questioning look, she explained, "Do you know how lucky you are?"

He shifted in his chair. "I mean, yeah."

"You can attend college anywhere you want. Your parents can afford it. Whereas I can only go to culinary school if I get a scholarship, which means I have to graduate with a 4.0. No exceptions. If I don't, I won't go anywhere."

Luke rubbed the back of his neck. "You wouldn't be able to go *anywhere?* I kinda doubt that."

"Okay, maybe I exaggerated. I wouldn't be able to go where I wanted. I could go to a community college or something." Jocelyn sighed. "But I don't want to do that. But you have all of these amazing choices."

"Not as many as you think. I still have to do what makes my parents happy. They keep a tight leash on me, especially with Tristan…" Luke stopped himself and shrugged.

Jocelyn had heard whispers about Luke's younger brother, but nothing definitive. Curiosity pressed her to ask, "What about him?"

"Have you done the Spanish homework yet?" said Luke. He wouldn't make eye contact with Jocelyn, either.

Luke never brought up Tristan again. Even when Jocelyn thought he was about to say something, he changed the subject. Whenever Jocelyn alluded to how annoying younger siblings were, Luke said nothing. It made no sense.

But Jocelyn had her own problems at home to deal with. Her dad had been working longer hours as of late, and Jocelyn rarely saw him. She made sure the bills were paid; she hadn't even asked her dad. She'd just started doing it. She made sure Alex did her homework, forged their dad's signature on anything he was supposed to sign, and kept the household running.

When a pipe burst under the sink during one especially cold night, Jocelyn was up in the middle of the night cleaning up the water. She knew enough how to turn the water off, but she didn't know what to do after that. Did she call a plumber? Their dad had always taken care of any household issues. He was a decent handyman.

But he was on a job site and wouldn't be home for another week. And they only had the one bathroom with the single sink.

The following afternoon, she struggled to stay awake in class all day. She'd been up all night trying to figure out how she could replace the pipe herself. But she couldn't figure out what type of pipe she'd need and how much it would cost.

"Jocelyn. Hey, Jocelyn!" Luke poked her. "You awake?"

Jocelyn opened her eyes. She'd nodded off during stretching. Ms. Tyson was coming her way now to tell her off for sleeping in class.

"Why are you so tired?" Luke peered at Jocelyn's face closely after PE had ended. "You look like crap."

Jocelyn scowled. "Just what every girl wants to hear. Thanks a lot."

"So why are you tired? Pull an all-nighter?"

Jocelyn didn't know why she told him, but on their way to lunch, she told him about the burst pipe, her dad being away, and her not being able to sleep. Luke listened without comment. When Jocelyn finished, he just said, "That sucks. I'm sorry."

Then he left her to go eat with his usual lunch buddies. Jocelyn felt hurt creeping into her chest, but she knew she was being stupid. What could Luke do about her problems, anyway?

She and Alex were eating dinner when the doorbell rang. Jocelyn got up and peered through the peephole to see Luke Wright on her doorstep.

"What are you doing here?" she said.

He was holding a plastic bag in one hand, a grin on his face. "I'm here to fix your pipe. Duh."

Then he came inside like he'd come to her house all the time. Alex, her eyes wide, didn't say a word as Luke walked past. Alex was *never* silent.

Jocelyn hurried after him, instantly embarrassed that the house was so messy. A hamper full of underwear sat in the hallway; Jocelyn chucked the whole thing into her room and shut the door before Luke could see it. The thought of him seeing her panties and bras was beyond humiliating.

"Do you really know what you're doing?" said Jocelyn as Luke got to work.

He shrugged a shoulder. "I watched some videos online. It didn't seem hard."

"That's not super reassuring."

He just grinned that stupid grin that made her heart flutter. But she was too tired to argue, so she let him try to fix the pipe. It was already broken. What was the worst that could happen?

In the living room, Alex, who'd just turned twelve, was smiling like a cat who'd caught the canary. "Is that your boyfriend?" she cooed.

Jocelyn snorted. "He's a friend."

"Suuuuuure. He was totally checking you out."

"Shut up and eat your food."

But Alex kept making little digs, especially when Luke would come back to the living room with questions. She'd waggle her eyebrows behind Luke's back and then begin singing under her breath, *Jocelyn and Luke, sitting in a tree…*

Luke managed to install a new pipe, although it took longer than Jocelyn would've thought. But when he proudly turned on the water for the faucet and no water came spurting below, Jocelyn felt warmth spread through her chest.

Words, dangerous words, hovered on her tongue. But she knew Alex was listening just around the corner. So she took Luke outside and gave Alex the look that said if she eavesdropped there would be hell to pay.

"Thank you," said Jocelyn, staring at her feet. "It was really nice of you to come by."

"I wanted to see you."

She couldn't look up. Her heart was pounding so hard

she felt dizzy. When Luke tilted her head up, she had to struggle to remember to breathe.

"What do you mean?" Jocelyn whispered.

"What do you think?"

Then he leaned down and kissed her.

THEY'D DATED FOR A MONTH. They'd kept it secret, mostly because Jocelyn knew her dad didn't want her to date in high school. Luke, though, hadn't tried to take their relationship public.

Looking back, Jocelyn knew why he'd been content to keep everything a secret.

They'd gone on dates to the few places on the island where people wouldn't see them. It'd been fun, discovering out-of-the-way spots where they could kiss and cuddle without prying eyes.

Jocelyn had fallen hard for the handsome boy with the kind eyes. When he'd given her a bouquet of roses one evening, she'd nearly blurted that she loved him.

But as with most things, it didn't last. Luke canceled one date. Then he took hours to respond to her texts. In PE, he avoided her, saying later that he didn't want to bring attention to her.

Jocelyn had believed him at first.

It had been the day before they would go on Thanksgiving break when Jocelyn had realized the truth. She'd been eating her lunch by herself when she'd wondered why she couldn't eat with Luke. She'd just be another person at the table. No one would suspect a thing.

She packed up her things and went to find him. He was in his usual seat, a group of four other students sitting around the table eating their lunches. Jocelyn didn't know most of them well, but she knew their names.

"Is this seat taken?" she said, pointing to a chair next to Luke.

Luke didn't even look at her. He just shrugged a shoulder and said, "Nope."

He didn't speak to her the entirety of lunch. Even when Jocelyn asked him about Spanish class, he ignored her. Jocelyn felt anger building inside her chest. When she had to swipe away tears, she abruptly stood up and walked away.

She confronted Luke after school. "What the hell is wrong with you?" she demanded.

She expected him to hug her, to tell her it'd all been an act. She'd misunderstood. He was keeping it secret for her benefit.

He did none of those things. "I think this thing has run its course," was all he said.

Jocelyn stared at him. "Are you breaking up with me?" she whispered.

That grin she'd loved was on his face now. But now she hated it because there was no laughter in it.

"Baby, did you think we were dating?" He chucked her under the chin. "Come on, we were just having a little fun. Don't take everything so seriously."

When Jocelyn had gotten home, she'd refused to let her dad inside even when he'd asked her why she was crying. Even Alex had left her alone. Jocelyn had cried and cried until she'd been sure she had no tears left.

Then in the morning, as she'd gazed at her red eyes, she'd told herself she'd hate Luke Wright for the rest of her life.

CHAPTER EIGHT

Luke had never considered himself the jealous type. He generally preferred to live and let live. If he wanted something another person had, he figured he'd just do the hard work to earn it.

Yet as he watched his friend Jack Benson kiss his fiancée, their faces bright with happiness, Luke's gut twisted.

He tossed back the last of his beer. He'd agreed to come to Jack and Gwen's place weeks prior for dinner. Luke almost wished he'd canceled tonight, but he pushed the thought aside.

Plastering a smile on his face, he entered the kitchen where the two lovebirds were trying to finish making dinner. They kept touching each other and laughing. Jack, a grumpy fisherman-turned-general-contractor not known for laughing at much of anything, seemed to smile and laugh all the time now. Gwen had turned him into a brand-new man.

"If you keep on like that," said Luke wryly, "we won't get to eat until midnight."

Gwen laughed. "You're probably right. You boys get out of here. I'll finish up here."

"We can help," both Luke and Jack said at the same time.

"I won't be offended if you go and talk while I'm in the kitchen." She waved a hand. "Go away. You're bothering me." But she belied the remark with a smile.

Jack and Luke sat in the comfortable living room, saying nothing for a while. Jack wasn't the chattiest of people, and Luke wasn't feeling like talking.

He hadn't said a word about the will, his inheritance, or his agreement with Jocelyn. Jack would probably tell him he'd lost his ever-loving mind.

Jack finally cleared his throat. "How's life?"

"You gotta be more specific, Benson."

Jack looked heavenward. "Aren't you the one who's usually asking the questions?"

"I just wanted to see if you could do it for once."

"Asshole."

That made Luke grin. "The family is fine. Work is fine. Everything is fine." *What a load of bullshit*, he thought to himself.

Jack was eyeing him, like he didn't believe Luke's words, either. "I'm sorry about your grandma. Did you get our card?"

"The card Gwen bought and you signed? Yeah, I did." Luke said more seriously, "She was an amazing lady. You would've liked her."

"Then I'm sorry I never met her."

Silence settled on them again. Luke forced himself to

stop wallowing in his own shit and ask, "How's work? And the restaurant?"

Jack had worked as a fisherman for over fifteen years, but with salmon getting scarcer every year in the region, he'd recently gotten his general contractor license. One of his first big projects was remodeling the house that had been turned into Gwen and Jocelyn's restaurant, Lyn's Eatery.

"Work is good. I like working with my hands. Although sometimes I miss being on the water. There's nothing like being out in the middle of the ocean, all by yourself." Jack's gaze went distant.

"But you got another boat, right?"

"Yeah, but with my work and Gwen's work, we don't go out much." Jack shrugged a shoulder. "The restaurant takes up a lot of her time."

"Too much of her time?" Luke pressed.

"Sometimes I feel like that, but you won't hear me saying it aloud." Jack sighed, setting his empty glass on the table in front of him. "If Gwen isn't dealing with staff being sick, she's dealing with Jocelyn harassing her sous chef. Gwen's had to deal with mediation more than once. I can tell she's exhausted."

At Jocelyn's name, Luke's ears perked up. "Mediation? What, are they fighting each other in the street?" he joked.

Jack didn't laugh. "The sous chef. What's her name… Kelly? She doesn't like Jocelyn. Or so Gwen says. To me, it sounds like stupid shit they should just hash out already."

Luke thought of Jocelyn, alone at the restaurant, working late into the night because her sous chef hadn't done her job. "Maybe she has a right to be frustrated," said Luke. "Jocelyn, I mean."

Jack gave him a strange look. "Never said she didn't. But you know Jocelyn. She's a hard-ass. I kinda doubt it's all one-sided."

"She works hard. Without her, the restaurant wouldn't exist. Haven't you heard everybody raving about the food? That's Jocelyn's doing."

Luke didn't know why he felt the need to defend her. Yet hearing Jack act like Jocelyn was simply being a petty jerk annoyed him.

Jocelyn Gray was a talented chef, and she deserved a sous chef who respected her and did the work she'd been hired to do.

"And without my fiancée, the place would've burned to the ground a week after opening. Jocelyn doesn't have the people skills Gwen does. She'd run people over without a second thought," said Jack. Now he looked like he was getting pissed. Then he added, "Since when do you care so much about Jocelyn? Doesn't she hate you?"

Luke scowled. "I don't care about *her*," he lied through his teeth. "I'm just playing devil's advocate. Ignore me."

Jack narrowed his eyes but just said, "I usually do."

Thankfully, they were interrupted when Gwen announced that dinner was ready. The conversation at the table was mostly about the restaurant, the bed and breakfast that Gwen also ran, and their upcoming wedding. To Luke's amusement, Jack was the one who talked most about the wedding.

"How many people are you inviting?" said Luke.

"It'll be pretty small. Just fifty or so," replied Gwen. Then she looked over at Jack with a raised eyebrow.

Jack was in the middle of chewing. He finally swallowed and then said, "Um, about that."

Luke raised an eyebrow, waiting.

"I wanted to ask if you'd be my best man."

Luke felt a bit like he'd been punched in the chest. Then, emotions he didn't want to analyze overmuch filled him. In a gruff voice, he said, "Of course I'll be your best man."

Jack looked relieved, while Gwen clapped her hands.

"He was so nervous about asking you," she said. "I told him you'd say yes. I thought he would've done it earlier while you two were alone…"

"I forgot," muttered Jack.

"In any case, here's to us, and to Luke for saying yes." Gwen raised her glass, Luke and Jack following suit.

After that, they talked more about the wedding, Luke discovering that although he'd agreed to be the best man, his friends didn't expect much of him.

"Are you saying I just have to wear a tuxedo and show up? No bachelor party or anything?" said Luke dubiously.

"Don't want one," was Jack's simple reply.

Luke glanced at Gwen. She put up her hands. "Don't look at me! He doesn't need my permission."

"Are you having a bachelorette party?" said Luke.

"Of course. Do you think Alex would let me not have one?" Gwen let out a laugh. "It'll be total insanity."

"No strippers," said Jack.

"Pretty sure there aren't any on the island. We'd have to import them, and that'd be expensive." Gwen wrinkled her nose. "Then again, this is Alex we're talking about. I'll make sure she knows for the thousandth time."

Talking about weddings, bachelorette parties, and everything in between made Luke want to confess his secret. But he and Jocelyn had agreed to keep it under wraps until they'd signed on the dotted lines. Besides, he knew his friends: they'd try to talk him out of it.

They'd tell him he couldn't marry someone he didn't love, that he'd be making the biggest mistake of his life. But they were madly in love. They didn't understand that sometimes, you had to make the hard choices.

Or, worse, they'd press him about his feelings for Jocelyn. The thought of that made him want to crawl under the table. No, he didn't need an inquisition into his *true* motives.

"I'm surprised you didn't run screaming from the room with us talking about wedding stuff," said Gwen after she'd brought in dessert.

"I'm not that much of a caveman," replied Luke. He bit into the warm brownie and added, "These are amazing."

"Thank you. They're Jocelyn's recipe. I can't take full credit for them."

Jack rumbled, "You made them."

"Oh, I can follow recipes, but I'm too chicken to just throw something together. Jocelyn can cook something without looking at a recipe, and it's always amazing."

Luke just kept eating his brownie. Jack was giving him a look again.

"Luke had a lot of things to say about Jocelyn earlier." Jack smirked when Luke glared at him. "Didn't you, buddy?"

Jack *never* called Luke "buddy." Clearly, Jack was out for blood. Or he just wanted to turn the screws a little tighter.

"I was just saying that I know Jocelyn can be a pain, but there's probably a reason for it," hedged Luke.

Gwen cocked her head to the side. "I thought you hated her." She tapped her chin. "No, wait, she hates *you* for some undisclosed reason. Do you know why, Luke?"

Luke kept his face carefully blank. He did know why, and her hatred was totally deserved.

"I'm not digging up ancient history," was all he said.

"Was that a yes? I think it was. Why are you two so cagey about this?" Gwen grinned. "Don't tell me she had your secret love child who she gave up for adoption or something."

Luke nearly choked on his brownie. He downed the rest of his water. "No children," he gasped out. "Christ, Gwen."

"Baby, don't give the man a stroke," said Jack.

"I'm kidding." Her eyes narrowed. "Then again, a little bird told me that he saw the two of you kissing in your office not too long ago…"

"Okay, well, I guess I'll head out." Luke stood up, his chair nearly toppling to the floor. He righted it just in time. "Thank you for dinner," he added quickly.

"I'll walk you out." Jack, sensing his friend was at the end of his rope, shot his fiancée a look that clearly said, *Leave the man alone.*

"Sorry," said Jack as they stood outside on the front steps. Night had already settled, the moon a silver crescent above them. "When Gwen gets on something, she's like a bloodhound."

"She's nosey."

Jack's lips twitched. "I'd tell you off, but I can't disagree."

Luke raked his fingers through his hair. "That kiss you saw that day—"

"Hey, man, it's your business—"

"It was nothing. We weren't thinking. I hadn't had sex in way too long and I guess she forgot who I was." Luke let out a tight laugh.

Jack didn't say anything. He just folded his arms across his chest.

The words *Jocelyn and I are getting married* nearly fell from Luke's tongue. If he'd drunk another beer, he probably would've spilled his guts. As it were, he bit his tongue just in time.

"You know, you two could hash out your differences," said Jack suddenly.

Luke stared. "What?"

"You and Jocelyn." His lips twitched again. "Gwen would love to mediate."

"Oh, Christ. Can you imagine? Pretty sure Jocelyn would tear my guts out if I asked."

At that, Jack just replied, "Maybe."

Luke drove home in silence, his mind buzzing. Up until this point, he'd felt nothing but determination in marrying Jocelyn. He needed his inheritance, after all. He had no choice.

But now, thinking about what would really happen after the wedding made him break out into a cold sweat. Sure, he could tell himself they'd agreed to the contract and would follow it no matter what. He knew Jocelyn, though. She wasn't going to make any of this easy for him.

As he parked his car outside his own place, he pressed his forehead to the steering wheel and groaned.

"You're a fucking idiot," he muttered to himself. "Idiot, idiot, *idiot*."

CHAPTER NINE

J ocelyn stared in the mirror, and for a split second, she didn't recognize the woman looking at her. It was her face, of course, but she looked pale, thin, and terrified.

She scowled at her reflection. She refused to show fear. This was her own choice, and she wasn't going to have a nervous breakdown right now.

Even if she was marrying Luke Wright in ten minutes, and none of her family or friends was in attendance. They couldn't be. She knew that, but it still hurt. Would her dad ever forgive her? Alex probably wouldn't, knowing her younger sister.

She hadn't told her best friend Bekah, either. So many nights, Jocelyn had been tempted. She'd even started the text that she'd send.

Hey, I'm getting married. Who? Oh, it doesn't matter.

I'm getting married to Luke Wright. No, he hasn't kidnapped me and forced me to the altar.

I'm in love with someone. You'd never guess who!

No, Bekah would definitely not believe any of those texts. She'd probably drive straight to Hazel Island to make sure Jocelyn was sane.

Would Bekah understand? Jocelyn chewed on her bottom lip, only to remember that doing so would smudge her lipstick. So she took to chewing on the inside of her cheek instead.

There was a knock on Jocelyn's door. She'd been given a suite of rooms right next to Luke's in the Wright mansion.

"Ready?" said Luke through the door.

Jocelyn swallowed. Getting up, she put her shoulders back, and before she could change her mind and run away, she opened the door to her fiancé.

THE CEREMONY WAS ATTENDED by Luke's parents as witnesses, along with the mysterious friend of Granny Esther's. The woman, who'd introduced herself as Opal earlier in the morning when she'd arrived, was inscrutable throughout the entire affair. Jocelyn wondered if the woman was just bored of the entire thing.

The vows, signing the marriage license, everything was done quickly and efficiently. Jocelyn had to take a deep breath before she signed her name on the license. She felt dizzy as she saw her signature next to Luke's.

"It's done," said Luke in a heavy voice. Jocelyn didn't know if he was talking to her or to himself.

Luke barely looked at Jocelyn. His kiss, when they'd been pronounced husband and wife, had been a mere peck on the lips. Jocelyn had been tempted to force him back down to redo the terrible, dry kiss.

"Congratulations," said Opal. A tiny woman, she barely came up to Jocelyn's shoulders. She was dressed immaculately, her rings and earrings probably worth a fortune.

"Thank you," said Jocelyn, trying to sound like she meant the words.

"Thank you for coming," said Luke.

Opal arched an eyebrow that looked tattooed on. "I'm surprised your mother would allow you to have a ceremony like this," she said to Luke. "The bride isn't even in white. Then again, perhaps that's for the best."

Jocelyn bristled. Luke put his arm around her, probably to restrain her. "We didn't want the publicity. Besides, spending money on a wedding seems ridiculous. It's just a single day."

"A single day that'll affect the rest of your life." Opal turned to Jocelyn. "Then again, perhaps it won't for you two. We shall see."

Opal went to speak with Luke's mom and dad. Jocelyn, when she saw that no one was looking, wrenched herself away from her new husband.

"Don't get pissy," said Luke.

Jocelyn swallowed the sharp retort on her tongue. Instead, she motioned him to a private corner and then said in a low voice, "You could at least seem like you *like* me."

"I married you." Based on his expression, he seemed to think that was all that was necessary.

"You were the one telling me we had to play things up for everyone. What was that kiss?"

Now Luke looked annoyed. "What, did you want me to bend you over my arm and give you a fairy-tale kiss?"

"No, but you could've at least seemed like you wanted to kiss me!"

They were both breathing hard now. Jocelyn realized too late that Luke was way too close—and that she was literally cornered.

"I was trying to be polite." His words were a growl. "I didn't want to make a spectacle. Being too obvious won't help us."

"There's a difference between being obvious and putting in basic effort!"

"I don't have time for this. We'll discuss this later."

Jocelyn scoffed. "What, at our weekly staff meeting?"

"I'll find a date and time for you on my calendar."

Jocelyn wasn't sure if he was being sarcastic or not. He stalked off before she could find out. She stood behind the curtain for a little while longer, rubbing her arms and trying to keep herself from crying.

She didn't know why she felt so near to tears. But something about Luke Wright turned her inside out. His rejections always eviscerated her. She hated it.

When Jocelyn felt calm enough, she emerged from her hiding place, only to nearly run into her new father-in-law. Gregory Wright grunted, putting a hand on her shoulder to steady them both.

Jocelyn apologized, feeling a blush heat her cheeks. She'd barely spoken to her father-in-law since she'd agreed to Luke's proposal. As far as she could tell, he was a proud, cold man who didn't seem all that interested in getting to know his son's new wife.

"Steady on," said Gregory. But he didn't move his hand from her shoulder.

Jocelyn stepped back. He noticed the movement, his lips quirking into a smile that was devoid of anything kind.

"I'm impressed," he said.

"Impressed?"

"With you. You saw an opportunity, and you seized it without a second thought." Gregory picked up a glass of gold-colored liquid from a nearby table. "Most women would have a few reservations, marrying a man in less than a month."

"Luke needed a wife. I'm helping him." Even as Jocelyn said the words, she knew they sounded halfhearted.

Gregory chuckled. "Come on, now. I'm not judging you. My wife and you are similar. You have ambitions. Nothing wrong with that."

"I didn't marry Luke just for his money."

Her father-in-law merely gazed at her in amusement. "You don't have to keep to the company line with me, darling."

The word darling felt like nails on a chalkboard to Jocelyn. Most of all, she hated that Gregory wasn't wrong.

She *had* married Luke for his money. But not for her own sake. She was doing it for her family.

"Excuse me," said Jocelyn. "Luke is probably looking for me."

"Just a moment." From behind her shoulder, Gregory said in a sinister voice, "Welcome to the family, *Mrs. Wright.*"

～

JOCELYN STAYED THE NIGHT, but not with Luke. She'd told her dad that she was going to Seattle to visit Bekah for the weekend. Alex would check in on him, along with caring for Fluffer at her place. That meant Jocelyn had two days before she had to face the music and face her family with what she'd done.

It was raining. Jocelyn stared at the large bow windows, listening to the rain patter against the glass. She couldn't sleep, even though she was exhausted. Her brain wouldn't turn off. She wished she'd brought something to help her sleep. She needed to keep her wits about her being in this house and with this family.

Hearing movement next door in Luke's rooms, she sat up. Her heart was in her throat when she heard a soft knock on the door that adjoined their bedrooms.

Of course this place has bedrooms made like this, she'd thought to herself upon seeing the door for the first time. *It wouldn't do for couples to actually sleep in the same bed.*

The knock sounded again. She was tempted to ignore it. But the feeling of loneliness was oppressive right then. She'd rather argue with her husband than stay in this huge bed by herself.

"Come in," she called out. Then she remembered that she was wearing her rattiest pajamas covered in flamingoes. Hardly wedding-night appropriate.

Did you want Luke to seduce you?

She wasn't entirely certain what her answer was to that.

"You're awake," said Luke. He wore a shirt and boxers, along with glasses. "It's late."

"You're awake, too," she pointed out.

"The rain." Luke gestured vaguely.

Jocelyn snorted. "You grew up in the Pacific Northwest and can't sleep when it rains? I find that hard to believe."

"It was thundering earlier."

"I heard one thunderclap. I didn't take you for such a weenie."

Luke came up to the bed and, before she could protest, got in beside her. She squawked in protest.

"Calm down. It's cold," he said as he tucked himself in.

Jocelyn was still sitting up, and she looked down at him lying in her bed with an incredulous expression.

"Were you *lonely?*" she questioned.

He turned to face her. "I told you: I couldn't sleep."

"Most people would just look at their phones, or read, or go get a snack."

"You're my wife. You're supposed to entertain me."

She gaped at him. "Entertain you? What, are you two years old?"

"Tell me a story." Even in the dim light, Jocelyn could see that his eyes were sparkling. "Help me fall asleep."

Jocelyn picked up a pillow and ominously hung it over his face. "I have a better way to get you to sleep."

But Luke grabbed the pillow so quickly that Jocelyn found herself pillow-less and then underneath him within a moment. He tossed the pillow aside and pinned her wrists to the bed.

"That wasn't very wifely of you," he said.

Jocelyn swallowed. His thighs were hairy and rubbed against her leg; his fingers were tight but not enough to hurt. Most of all, she could feel a growing hardness against her hip that made her want to squirm.

"I'm your wife in name only," she whispered.

Luke leaned down. Their lips were a breath apart. "I could have you naked and screaming my name in five minutes."

Any retorts Jocelyn might've come up with fell from her lips. She couldn't breathe. Her body felt like a fuse had been lit inside it. She could barely keep herself from kissing him—kissing him like she'd wanted to be kissed after the ceremony.

"I'm sorry about the kiss," he said, as if reading her mind. He hadn't moved away yet. "I should've done better. I just didn't want to embarrass you."

"I'm not that delicate."

"I think you're more delicate than you'd ever admit." Luke leaned up so he could gaze into her eyes. "I think you were hurt. I think you want me to treat you more like a wife." He punctuated the remark with a touch just below her breast.

She sucked in a breath. "We said no sex," she blurted.

He grinned, but it was a predatory grin. "We never said no touching, though. In fact, I'm pretty sure we talked about doing all kinds of touching."

He brushed his fingers below her breast. Jocelyn felt her nipple peak, and she bit her lip to restrain a moan. "Pretty sure," she panted, "that it's supposed to be in front of other people."

"I could always call my parents to come in here."

Jocelyn choked. Luke laughed and then rolled off her. She hit him on the shoulder with a pillow.

"I'm going to bed." He got up but leaned down to kiss Jocelyn.

"I thought you wanted to sleep together." She hated that she sounded disappointed.

"And not fuck you senseless? I'd recommend locking your door."

He kissed her one last time and disappeared back into his room.

CHAPTER TEN

Luke realized too late he'd created his own version of hell.

With Jocelyn just next door, it was sheer torture not to return to her bed. He'd only gone into her bedroom because…he didn't know. Had it been because he'd been lonely, as Jocelyn had said?

He scowled in the dark. His cock was still hard, and his body seemed to always be at the ready whenever his wife was near.

His wife. The words sent a frisson of heat through. Heat —and sheer terror.

He eventually fell asleep, despite the rain and the knowledge that Jocelyn lay only a few yards away. But his dreams were full of erotic images, where he hadn't left Jocelyn's bed and had seduced her just as he'd threatened to do.

When he awoke, he was still exhausted, his head hurt, and he barely restrained himself from growling at everyone he met.

Luke avoided his wife. Was it kind? No. Did he fell guilt over it? Of course.

But he told himself he was protecting her. She'd been very clear that she wanted to keep their marriage platonic. Luke didn't trust himself when it came to Jocelyn. He'd kissed her at the ceremony like that because he would've plunged his tongue and felt her up in five seconds flat.

Luke snorted, sitting in his office by himself that morning. He adjusted himself, too. Christ, he needed to get his head on straight. This was not the time to let his hormones take over. He'd end up with a knife in his heart—whether literally or metaphorically, he wasn't sure.

Dinner was a tense affair. His parents barely spoke; Jocelyn stared at her plate the entire evening. Luke was too irritable to attempt conversation. It was a pathetic scene. When they'd all finished, Luke had left without another word.

That night—the last night Jocelyn would be at the house until she settled things with her dad—Luke once again lay awake in the dark. He didn't even have the sound of the rain keeping him awake this time.

He must've dozed off, though, because he came awake suddenly to the sound of a scream. He reacted without thinking. He burst into Jocelyn's dark bedroom. A figure ran toward him and collided straight into his chest.

Luke fumbled for a light. He hadn't put his glasses on in his haste to get inside, so it took him a second to find the switch.

"What the hell?" he said to Jocelyn after he'd gone around the room to make sure no one else was in there. "Why were you screaming?"

Jocelyn was rubbing her arms. She wouldn't look at him.

"Did you have a nightmare?" He softened his voice.

Jocelyn wrinkled her nose. "Sure. A nightmare."

He gave her a strange look. "So it was, or it wasn't?"

Sighing, she moved to stand next to her bed. The covers were all pushed to the foot of the bed, the plethora of pillows on the floor. She began to replace the pillows.

"Promise you won't laugh at me," she said.

She seemed so serious that Luke had to force himself not to smile. "Okay. I won't laugh."

"There was a spider."

"A spider?"

Jocelyn huffed. "Yes, I felt something crawling on my face. At first I thought it was a dream, but then I felt *legs*. Legs!" She shuddered.

Luke wished he hadn't promised not to laugh. She looked so put out by the sheer rudeness of a spider crawling on her. It was adorable.

"I didn't know you were afraid of spiders," he said, his voice choked.

"I'm not, as a rule. I usually leave them alone. But it was crawling on me!"

"I'm sorry. That was very rude of it."

She narrowed her eyes at him. "Now you're making fun of me."

"I would never."

Rolling her eyes, she got into bed, but not before she checked for the spider in question in the sheets. "You can go," she said to Luke. "Turn off the light before you go."

Luke's mind had wandered from the spider attack to the

fact that his darling wife was wearing very short shorts and a very revealing tank top at the moment. And based on how visible her nipples were, she wasn't wearing a bra.

Jocelyn caught him staring at her breasts. She pulled the flat sheet to cover them. "Stop ogling and go away."

"I'm admiring," he replied. He found himself going to her bed instead of to his own. He did, however, turn off the light first.

"What are you doing?" Her words were a whisper.

"Admiring," he repeated.

"You can't see anything now."

"I can admire with my fingers."

He punctuated his remark with touching her shoulder, running his fingers down her arm.

"I can use my mouth." He kissed her neck. "And my nose." He inhaled the scent of her skin. Lemony, he thought. As bright and sharp as Jocelyn was.

She was breathing hard now. When Luke pushed the offending sheet down, she didn't protest. He kissed her between her breasts.

Jocelyn curled her fingers in his hair. "Luke," she moaned. "What are you doing?"

He glanced up at her. "Do I really need to explain?" Tweaking a nipple, he grinned when she inhaled sharply.

"Oh, shut up," were her last words because all speech seemed to disappear from her.

Luke kissed and caressed her breasts, wishing he could turn the light back on to see them in their full glory. They were small but plump, the perfect handful. He'd always been a breast man, he had to admit. And his wife seemed to enjoy how much attention he gave them.

He sucked her nipples in between tweaking and pulling them. He listened to her gasps, or how her body arched at certain touches.

Soon enough, Jocelyn was under him, and he was kissing her mouth. She responded with equal fervor, which only sent his own desire into overdrive.

Any doubts he pushed to the side. She was his wife. He had a right to touch her, to make her his.

He pushed her tank top down her arms before he delved beneath the band of her pajama shorts. Pressing his palm against her mound, he smiled when she groaned.

"Luke," she whispered.

She repeated his name as he pushed the panel of panties aside to dip a finger between her folds. He spread her moisture, loving how responsive she was to him. As he gently played with her, he kept kissing her with a similarly lazy rhythm.

Jocelyn arched when his thumb brushed her clit.

"Do you want me to make you come?" He rasped the words in her ear.

She nodded eagerly. "You're going to kill me."

That made him laugh. Tugging at her ear with his teeth, he pressed a finger inside her tight sheath as he began to rub her in just the right spot. Her hips kept pushing at him; he lay on top of her to keep her from wiggling away.

"Tell me how much you want me," he whispered.

She was panting against his neck. "Please," she begged.

He added another finger inside her. It took only a few more strokes of his thumb on her clit to make her orgasm. He captured the sound of her loud groan with a kiss as she bucked and arched under him. Her body shook until she collapsed in an exhausted heap.

Luke pulled her into an embrace, her back to his front. They were both sweaty and breathing hard.

Jocelyn eventually reached behind her to rub his cock through his boxers. Luke gritted his teeth.

"Baby, you don't have to," he said, even as he desperately wanted her to keep going.

He could feel Jocelyn smiling. Flipping over, she pushed his boxers down to stroke his cock, her grip firm. She licked at his lips, and Luke was more than happy to continue kissing her.

His own release was already close. As she tightened her grip and swirled her thumb over the tip of his cock, he saw stars behind his eyelids. Then he came with rapid spurts, cursing as pleasure racked his body.

"Fuck," said Luke into Jocelyn's neck.

"Yeah. I know." Her voice was soft.

Luke didn't want to think too deeply about the feelings swirling inside him. They'd just had some fun—nothing more, nothing less.

But as Jocelyn fell asleep in his arms, he couldn't deny how right it felt, either.

When Luke awoke the next morning, he was alone. Reaching out, he found nothing but cold sheets.

He heard movement in Jocelyn's bathroom. Yawning, he found her already dressed. Based on the steam still on the mirror, she'd showered, too.

"Good morning," he rumbled, hugging her from behind. "How did you sleep?"

Jocelyn stiffened. "Fine."

Luke's good mood soured when she wriggled free of his grasp. She didn't say anything else, instead focusing on brushing her hair and putting it into a ponytail.

"I'll be heading out within the hour," said Jocelyn. She met Luke's eyes in the mirror. "I have to get to work."

"Ah. Work."

"And I have to pick up my rabbit from my sister's. Also check in on my dad." She grimaced. "I'll need a cover story. I told him I was seeing Bekah in Seattle. I guess I'll just have to make something up."

Luke crossed his arms. "Or you could just tell him the truth."

"I'm going to. I'm going to tell everybody." Jocelyn scowled when her hair refused to cooperate. "Sometimes I just want shave my damn head."

Luke took the brush from her. He pulled the hair tie from her hair, letting the blond locks fall to her shoulders. "Why do you always put it up?"

"Loose hair isn't a good idea in a kitchen."

"You aren't in a kitchen twenty-four seven."

Luke pushed her hair to the side so he could kiss the nape of her neck. He smiled when he felt her shiver.

"Did last night freak you out?" he said quietly.

Now she wouldn't meet his gaze. "No."

"Liar."

She stiffened against him. This time, he wrapped an arm around her waist and wouldn't let her go.

"Don't let yourself overthink things. It was just some

good fun. We have chemistry. There's nothing wrong with that," he said.

"It complicates things."

"It doesn't have to."

"Oh, like it's so easy. You can't avoid getting burned if you willingly stick your hand in a fire."

"Are you saying I'm going to get you burned?"

Her voice was so soft he barely heard it. "If I'm not careful, yeah."

She broke free of his embrace and hurried past him. One half of him wanted to keep her in his arms, while the other knew he should let her be. Besides, he'd be an idiot if he let himself think this marriage was real.

He'd married her for his inheritance. This wasn't about love. He knew that, yet it didn't stop him from wanting her again. It didn't stop him from wanting to protect her, either.

"When will you be back?" said Luke as he watched Jocelyn zip up her travel bag.

"I'm not sure." She swallowed. "I know we talked about having my dad move into a place next to us, but as I thought about it, it'd be easier if he could stay in his house. I could see him every day, and if not, Alex could help. But I do worry if something happens at night. What if he falls or he has another stroke when I'm not there?"

Luke's frustration with the situation melted in the face of Jocelyn's fear. He took her hands. "What about hiring a nurse?"

"That'd be expensive."

"So would moving your dad to a new place."

She licked her lips. "I'll think about it. I'm not sure it's necessary, to be honest. If he had an alarm to call for help if he needed…"

"Then we'll talk to his doctor. Together we all make a plan that's best for him."

Tears shimmered in Jocelyn's eyes. To Luke's surprise, she threw her arms around him. "Thank you," she said into his shoulder.

"Of course." He kissed the top of her head. "Anything for my wife," said Luke in a resigned voice.

CHAPTER ELEVEN

When Gwen stared at Jocelyn in complete shock for what felt like eternity, Jocelyn wondered if she'd broken her friend's brain.

"You're kidding," said Gwen finally. "Please tell me you're kidding."

Jocelyn grimaced. "I'm not kidding."

"This isn't some elaborate prank?" Gwen opened her office door to peek out into the hallway. When no one yelled SURPRISE, she began to look for hidden cameras instead.

"It's not a joke," said Jocelyn, exasperated now. "Luke and I got married. I know it's sudden—"

"Sudden! Sudden is one thing. But you hate him. *Hate him.* Why would you marry him?" Gwen slowly sat down in her chair. "It makes zero sense."

"You don't have to understand why we did it."

That made Gwen frown. "Are you in trouble?" She glanced at Jocelyn's midriff. "Is there another reason…?"

"I'm not pregnant. Besides, there's no reason to get married nowadays just for that."

Gwen shrugged. "It still happens. I have a feeling Luke wouldn't be the type to let a woman have his kid without his involvement. Jack would probably drag me to the altar if I got pregnant right now. Some guys are like that."

"You're already engaged, though."

Gwen smiled. "I think it's just a caveman-instinct thing. Don't ask me how guys' minds work."

Jocelyn sat down heavily in the chair across from Gwen. "There's no baby," she repeated. *Kinda hard to get pregnant if you're not having sex*, her mind said wryly. "We just wanted to get married." Swallowing, Jocelyn added, "We're in love."

That made Gwen laugh. Laugh! Jocelyn's face heated.

"Oh, you're serious." Gwen hurried around to take Jocelyn's hands. "I'm sorry. I really thought you were kidding. I just find it hard to believe you could go from hating Luke to loving him and then marrying him—"

"Love and hate are two sides of the same coin."

When Gwen remained unconvinced, Jocelyn pulled out the plain gold band that was her wedding ring. She put it on her left hand. "Do you believe me now?"

"It wasn't about believing you, but believing why you did it."

Jocelyn looked at the ring: it was simple, but it had an inscription with Luke and Jocelyn's initials. When Jocelyn had noticed the detail at the ceremony, she'd been hit with so many conflicting feelings that she'd almost wanted to throw the ring across the room.

"Be that as it may…" Gwen let Jocelyn's hand go, but not before she gazed at the plain gold band on her left ring finger. "You'd tell me if you were in trouble, right?"

Jocelyn wanted to sink into the floor. She hated when

anyone tried to get her to be vulnerable. It made her stomach twist.

"I can take care of myself. Don't worry," she said finally.

Gwen raised an eyebrow. "I know you can, but it doesn't mean you have to. Nobody is an island." She chuckled. "Even if we live on one."

There was a knock on Gwen's office door, and a familiar voice said, "Gwen, are you in there?"

"Oh, it's Felicity. I'd forgotten we'd agreed to get lunch today." Gwen shot Jocelyn a look. "I can ask for a rain check, though."

Jocelyn stood. "No, don't cancel because of me."

Jocelyn tried her best to avoid speaking with Felicity. Not that she disliked the girl, but she was also good friends with Alex, although the two were completely opposite in terms of personalities.

Felicity Linden was a pretty girl, but you could hardly tell, since she tended to keep her hair in front of her face. She had a large, wine-stained birthmark on her left cheek from her temple to her jaw. She was soft-spoken and shy. Jocelyn had never gotten her to say more than a few words in her presence. She had a feeling the girl was terrified of her.

"Oh, Jocelyn," said Felicity. "Nice to see you."

Jocelyn gave an awkward wave. "I was just heading to the restaurant."

Felicity glanced at Jocelyn's hand, and her eyes widened. Jocelyn realized too late that she'd waved with her left hand —the one still wearing her wedding band.

She sighed and said, "Close the door behind you, will you?"

Jocelyn knew she was a coward. Despite having been back at home with her dad for three days, she'd yet to tell him about marrying Luke.

Her dad, though, rarely left the house, so it was unlikely he'd find out from someone else, despite both Gwen and Felicity now knowing about the marriage. Jocelyn trusted that they'd keep her secret.

As far as telling Alex, Jocelyn was avoiding her, too. She didn't need her younger sister's judgmental remarks at the moment.

Luke texted her every day, asking her if she'd told her family yet. Jocelyn simply replied that she wanted to find the right time. Based on Luke's curt replies, he wasn't too happy about her continuing to delay the inevitable.

After a long day at work, Jocelyn came home to find her dad in the kitchen cooking. "Go sit down," said Pete when Jocelyn poked her head into the kitchen. "You look tired."

She was tired. He had no idea.

Pete made his famous dish of rice and beans—the one thing he could cook—and they both ate in companionable silence. In her pocket was her wedding ring, and it felt like a brand that kept getting hotter and hotter the longer she waited.

Finally, Jocelyn went to sit on the ottoman so she faced her dad. She pulled the ring from her pocket. "I have some-thing to tell you," she said.

Pete took the ring. "What's this?"

"It's a wedding ring."

Pete was turning over the ring, his eyes narrowed as he

read the inscription. "Is that an L? And a J? Did you find this somewhere?"

"No, it's mine." She swallowed against the lump in her throat. "I got married a few days ago, Dad."

Her dad simply kept turning the ring over and over. Then he returned it to her with a shake of his head. "Not right now, Joss. I'm tired."

Jocelyn's heart twisted. "Dad, I got married. To Luke Wright. I know it's sudden, and I'm sorry you weren't there, but we wanted to elope—"

Pete was looking at the TV over Jocelyn's shoulder. To her shock, she could see tears in his eyes. Guilt filled her; she felt like she was going to throw up.

"I'm tired," he repeated. "Let's just watch TV for tonight."

The speech Jocelyn had rehearsed for days dried up inside her throat. She'd expected surprise, even anger, but this? It was as if her dad simply couldn't comprehend what she'd done.

"I'm not leaving you," said Jocelyn, her voice breaking. "I'll be moving in with Luke, but we can hire a nurse for you, and I'll still come to see you as much as possible. Alex, too. You'll get to stay in the house—"

"Jocelyn Diane." Her dad's voice was sharp, sharper than she'd ever heard it. "I don't want to talk about it."

Jocelyn sat in silence the rest of the evening, swiping at stray tears. When she got up and began to pack, Fluffer hopping after her, Pete said nothing.

"I'll be staying with Luke tonight," she said twenty minutes later. She had Fluffer in a carrier as well. "I'll stop by in the morning before work."

Pete said nothing. Jocelyn bit her lip and walked out.

THE FOLLOWING MORNING, Jocelyn stopped by her dad's place as she'd promised. But to her surprise, she found Alex waiting outside.

"Is it true?" said Alex, her cheeks flushed. "Did you marry Luke Wright?"

Jocelyn's shoulders drooped. "Let's talk in my car."

"I'm not going to make a scene."

But Alex followed Jocelyn to her car and climbed into the passenger seat without further protest. Her arms crossed, Alex had her chin to her chest.

"Is it true?" asked Alex quietly.

"Who told you?"

"Oh, a little bird told me. But I told that person it couldn't be true. There was no way. Because you're my sister, and you would've said something before Judy fucking Turner would find out." Alex gaze caught Jocelyn's. "Right?"

"I was going to tell you—"

"What, when you and Luke had five kids and a joint checking account?"

Jocelyn's head started pounding. "I don't need this from you right now. Everything is a mess, okay? I told Dad, and he refused to talk about it. He iced me out. He's never, ever done that before."

Alex was quiet at that pronouncement. To Jocelyn's shock, she realized that her sister's lip was wobbling.

"Do you know how humiliating it was," whispered Alex,

"to hear the news that my sister got married from some random person? That you didn't think I mattered enough to know? Or, God forbid, attend the stupid ceremony?"

"No one was invited. We eloped."

Alex swiped at her tears. "That only makes me feel a little bit better."

"Look, I was going to tell you. I don't know how Judy of all people found out. I know Gwen and Felicity wouldn't have said anything—"

"They knew before me?" Alex's voice was raised now.

Jocelyn wanted to crawl under a rock and die. "It wasn't planned, Alex. It just happened."

"No, it's fine. I get it. You have your life, and I have mine. It's fine. Don't worry about it."

Frustration made Jocelyn snap, "Will you stop making this about you? I'm dealing with a huge mountain of shit at the moment. I don't have time to deal with your tantrums. I'm the one who always has to take care of this family. So forgive me if I don't always include you in every decision I make."

Alex stilled. The silence in the car was deafening now. Jocelyn was gripping the steering wheel so hard her joints ached.

"You think I'm just a stupid kid, don't you?" said Alex. "I'm still that irresponsible teenager who you couldn't control."

"Alex, I don't have time for this—"

"Well, you're going to hear it now. I know I'm a fuck-up, but you don't have to keep reminding me, either. You never want to support me. You've wanted to keep me in a cage because it makes you feel better. You want me to stay your naive little sister you can boss around. Did you ever think that treating me like I'm stupid isn't helping anyone?"

Jocelyn stared at her sister in shock. "Anything I've done in the past I've done to protect you."

"Protect me? Come on. When you got me kicked off the dance team, you did it out of revenge. Not because you cared about my future. If you did, you wouldn't have done something so cruel."

"Now you're just bringing up ancient history. Get over it, Alex."

Alex smiled, but it was a sad smile. "Is that your strategy for life? 'Just get over it'? You can't bury your feelings forever. They'll come for you eventually."

Jocelyn glanced at the time. She needed to go to work. "Can you check on Dad?" she said.

"Yeah. Whatever you need."

Jocelyn flinched at her sister's sarcasm. She watched Alex go into the house and then put her head in her hands. She wished she could call in sick, but there was no way Kelly could handle everything without Jocelyn.

But she struggled to focus all day. She couldn't stop thinking about what Alex had said.

For so many years, Jocelyn had always seen her sister as selfish and immature. Jocelyn had had to be both her older sister and her mom, and she realized in a moment of clarity that she'd probably resented the role.

It hadn't helped that Alex had rebelled—hard. She'd begun hanging out with the wrong crowd in junior high, experimenting with booze and pot. When Jocelyn had found out, she'd grounded her sister and had forbidden her to see her friends.

But Jocelyn had been all of eighteen. She hadn't known what she was doing. And their dad had been too busy with work to notice. Jocelyn had tried to confide in him, but he'd just tell her she needed to fill the place that their mother had left when she'd abandoned her family.

As Jocelyn had gotten harder on her sister, Alex had gotten better at sneaking around. It was as if every time Jocelyn tried to keep Alex close, Alex found a way to wriggle free. They would get into explosive fights: screaming, insults, and slammed doors.

After graduating from high school, Jocelyn had remained at home for two years. She'd gotten a scholarship from the University of Washington, but then their dad had gotten injured at a job site. Jocelyn had ended up deciding to stay to help him and to keep an eye on her sister.

When Alex was fifteen, she started dating an older boy —a senior to her freshman. Jocelyn had disapproved, which had only given Alex more of a reason to keep dating him.

At the same time, Alex had made the dance team, which, despite their high school's small size, was one of the best in the state. As a freshman, it was a huge deal that Alex had been selected.

Yet Alex kept sneaking out, to Jocelyn's dismay. One night, Jocelyn stayed up all night, confronting her sister when she climbed through her bedroom window right before sunrise.

That'd resulted in another vicious fight. Their dad had to break it up and order Jocelyn to her own room.

When Jocelyn found condoms in her sister's drawer, though, fear made her impulsive. It wasn't that she didn't think teenagers shouldn't have sex, but Alex's boyfriend was legally an adult. Alex didn't know what she was getting herself into.

So Jocelyn did what she thought she had to do: she told Alex's dance coach about her drinking, the pot-smoking, even dating a senior.

Within a few days, Alex had been kicked off the team. They had a zero-tolerance policy for underage drinking or drugs, which Jocelyn had known. Then she'd reported Alex's boyfriend to the cops.

Alex had never found out who'd reported her boyfriend, but she'd figured out who'd reported her to her coach quickly enough. She'd then given Jocelyn the silent treatment for three months until Jocelyn left for culinary school.

Jocelyn had never regretted what she'd done. She'd been protecting her sister as best she'd could. But had she gone too far? Had she done it as one last-ditch effort to control her unruly sister under the guise of being protective?

Jocelyn was all out of sorts when she arrived at Luke's after dinner service. He was staying at his own place now, for which Jocelyn was thankful. She didn't have any interest in being around his parents right now.

But Luke wasn't here. Jocelyn let Fluffer out of his cage, kissing the top of his soft head. "It's just you and me, buddy," she whispered.

Of course, when it rained, it poured. Before Jocelyn could even drink a glass of wine, she received a text from Bekah.

Call me. Now.

CHAPTER TWELVE

Luke had always assumed that when he got married, his wife would be, well, *around.* He'd see her in the morning before they went to work. He'd see her in the evenings when they came home. They'd spend weekends together, or at least a few hours sitting together binge-watching some TV show.

But despite having gotten married two weeks ago, Luke barely saw Jocelyn. She was up at the crack of dawn, and she came home by nine or ten p.m. She was either working or seeing her dad.

Luke should've been fine with the arrangement. They weren't really *married*, in the true sense of the word. They weren't even sharing a bedroom, for God's sake. Now that she'd moved into his own apartment, Luke would've thought the forced proximity would've created more opportunities to get to know each other.

At the very least, he should be feeling like she was too present. Annoyed that she left hair in the bathroom sink or the toothpaste cap unscrewed. Maybe she even put the toilet paper roll on the wrong way.

But no, Jocelyn didn't do any of those things. If not for her clothes—and her rabbit, who Luke didn't fully understand why anyone would own one—he'd never know she'd moved in.

Luke threw himself into work. He'd begun expanding his portfolio of investing in various small businesses, including backing Lyn's Eatery. Although Luke had been skeptical of opening yet another restaurant on Hazel Island, the business seemed to be thriving so far. But he also knew that it wouldn't be the shiny new thing forever. Restaurants often found themselves closing their doors when they became old news.

He also had more personal projects, including a small company that was pushing for legislation that would protect salmon populations around the island. Due to both over-fishing and global warming, many fishermen and -women had been forced to abandon their livelihoods, including Jack.

Luke had become passionate about the local ecosystem on Hazel Island when he'd first learned about it back when he was a teenager.

Of course, to really make an effect, Luke needed money —his inheritance, more importantly.

It was midday on Sunday when Luke decided he was tired of the silence of his apartment. He wished Jocelyn had brought some loud dog or obnoxious cat with her instead of a silent rabbit. He stopped to gaze at her rabbit, who was munching on hay and hardly seemed to notice Luke's appearance.

"Never got the point of owning rodents," said Luke.

Fluffer wiggled his nose and kept eating, unbothered.

When Luke arrived at Lyn's, it was packed. It was brunchtime, and they'd already become a popular spot for both islanders and tourists. The restaurant was loud and bustling, waitstaff sidling through tables and people with huge trays of plates like they were made of liquid.

"How many?" the hostess, a girl Luke didn't recognize, asked him.

"I'm here to see Jocelyn."

The girl's eyes widened. "Oh. Um, she's in the kitchen, probably."

Luke could hear the whispers starting as he went toward the back. The news that he and Jocelyn had married had spread like wildfire. Luke, though, had mostly avoided people since the ceremony.

"Oh, Luke!" A middle-aged woman stopped him with a light arm touch. "I heard the happy news! Congratulations! Tell your mom I said hi."

Luke had no idea who this woman was, but he promised to tell his mom she said hello. He soon found himself stopped by one person after another, wishing him well or saying something sly about him marrying so secretly. A few were put out that they hadn't been invited.

By the time Luke walked into the kitchen, he wanted to find a private corner to decompress. *Should've slipped in through the back*, he thought to himself.

But he was soon distracted when he spotted Jocelyn. She was moving with almost un-humanlike speed, flipping an order in one skillet while checking another that was in the oven. She gave orders and yelled for this ingredient or that.

Luke folded his arms and simply watched his wife. She was clearly in her element. She moved with a confidence that Luke couldn't help but find unbearably sexy. Despite her blond hair covered in a chef's cap, a sheen of sweat on her forehead, and her hands stained with red—had she been cutting beets?—she was still attractive to him.

His silent watch was soon interrupted when one of the cooks noticed him. Then others noticed, and finally Jocelyn glanced over her shoulder and saw him.

For a moment, the entire kitchen seemed frozen in time. Luke wondered if he touched one of them, if they'd explode into a million pieces. Clearing his throat, he said, "Good morning."

Titters erupted from two of the waitstaff picking up orders. Another woman, younger than Jocelyn, had a smirk on her face. Luke had a feeling this was the infamous sous chef Kelly.

"Luke." Jocelyn hurried toward him, then turned to her staff to say, "Get back to work."

The staff snapped into motion once again. Jocelyn took his arm and led him to the hallway. "What is it?"

"Can't a husband say hello to his wife while she's at work?"

"I'm busy."

"They'll be fine without you for a few minutes."

Jocelyn muttered, "So you think."

Luke stared down at his wife, suddenly not sure what he wanted to say. Had he come here just to say good morning? Or had he actually *missed* her?

Based on how Jocelyn kept glancing back at the kitchen, she wasn't at all interested in why he'd come.

"You haven't been home much," he said.

She cocked her head to the side. "I've been busy."

"So I came to see you, instead."

Her eyes widened. She tucked a piece of hair behind her ear. "Um, okay."

"But why do I get the feeling you've been avoiding me, too?"

She wouldn't look at him now. "I have a lot going on."

Luke tilted her chin up so she had to look at him. "We're never going to convince anyone we're really married if we never see each other."

"Plenty of couples work full-time."

"Not newlyweds supposedly madly in love."

Jocelyn pushed his hand away. "Look, I can try to get home earlier, but there's no guarantee. Things are complicated right now."

"That's all that I ask."

Before she could slip away, he kissed her. She froze, her eyes still open, but when he slipped his tongue into her mouth, she melted. He loved that he could make her melt so easily. He wrapped an arm around her waist and kissed her like he'd been dying to since that night at the mansion.

Someone made a noise. Luke didn't end the kiss right then, though. He slowly broke their embrace and didn't even look at who'd interrupted them.

"Um, sorry," said a male voice. His voice squeaked as he said the last syllable. "I'll just…"

The guy scurried off before Jocelyn could respond. Luke laughed, which made her slap him on the arm.

"Great, now they're all going to gossip about this," she said, clearly annoyed.

"That's exactly what we want, though."

She blinked, then ducked under his arm with a huff. Luke just chuckled under his breath. And he got to watch her ass bounce as she walked, so that was a plus.

Luke's stomach rumbled. He realized he was actually starving. Using both a combination of his charm and his status as the head chef's handsome new husband, he finagled getting a table without waiting for too long.

When the waitress came up to take his order, he said, "I'd like to talk to the head chef directly."

The girl stuttered out a reply and hurried away. Luke drummed his fingers on the table, wondering if Jocelyn would actually come if summoned.

She did, but she didn't look happy about it. "What do you want *now?*"

"I wanted you to make me something off the menu. Let your creativity shine."

She put her hands on her hips. "I don't have time for whatever it is you're trying to do."

"I told you: I want you to make me something special." Luke grinned. "I'm a paying customer, aren't I?"

Sighing, Jocelyn nodded and returned to the kitchen. Luke had a feeling she'd only agreed in order not to make a scene.

And really, he wanted to see what she could make on the fly. Knowing her, she'd enjoy it—if she let herself, that is.

Twenty minutes later, the waitress returned with his dish: poached eggs on sourdough toast with garlicky greens and cheesy grits.

"Compliments of the chef," the girl said. "Can I get you anything else?"

"No. This looks great."

Luke savored every single bite: the egg was perfectly cooked, the yolk delightfully runny. The hint of spice along with the fresh herbs elevated the dish. The bread was lightly toasted, sea salt coating the sides. The grits were cheesy heaven. Along with the greens, Luke was in heaven. Despite what seemed like a simple dish, all of the components complemented each other.

Luke barely restrained himself from licking his plate when he'd finished. He'd never eaten something that good before. And it was just eggs, toast, and grits, with some greens! His wife was a damn genius.

Luke had just paid the bill when, to his surprise, his best friend Jack Benson sat down across from him. Based on Jack's narrowed eyes and clenched jaw, the man was not in a good mood.

"Hullo, Jack. Nice to see you."

Jack just looked at the ring on Luke's finger. "Interesting news, Wright."

"Oh, this? Yeah, it just happened. Congratulate us."

"I'd rather not."

Luke took a drink of his water, tension filling him. He could tell Jack was pissed at him.

"Look, I would've invited you to the wedding, but we eloped. Only my parents were there, and nobody else. Don't be mad at me," said Luke, trying to sound lighthearted.

"Do you think this is because you didn't invite me?" Jack looked incredulous. "I don't give a fuck about your wedding, man. I want to know what the hell you're doing getting married to Jocelyn Gray of all people."

"I know you don't like her—"

"Never said that—"

"But we wanted to do it. We're in love." Luke shot Jack a sly look. "Just like you and Gwen are. I know you wish you could run off to the courthouse instead of messing with wedding shit."

Jack stared at him, assessing him. Luke knew that Jack could smell bullshit from a mile away, like a damn bloodhound.

"What I don't understand," said Jack in a quiet voice, "is how you got her to agree. Everybody on the island knows she hates you. She'd never have said yes unless there was a reason."

"I told you: she loves me."

"Bullshit." Jack slapped a hand down onto the table, making Luke's glass nearly fall over. "You did something, told her something, cornered her somehow—"

"Is this what this is about? You think you need to look out for Jocelyn from me, the big bad wolf?"

"She doesn't have anyone to look out for her. Gwen and I realized this a long time ago. Her dad is sick, and her sister is a mess. And yeah, I might not always agree with how she runs her kitchen, but I respect her. And my fiancée considers her a friend, which makes her *my* friend."

Jack leaned closer, his voice so low that Luke had to strain to hear him over the noise of the restaurant. "I don't know what you're on about, but if you hurt Jocelyn, you hurt Gwen. And if you hurt Gwen, I'll break your fucking kneecaps."

Luke wanted to laugh, but he knew Jack. Jack didn't make idle threats.

"Do you feel better?" joked Luke, leaning back.

"Can you take anything seriously?"

Luke put up a hand. "Don't flip the table. I hear you." Scowling, he added, "Although I want to punch you in the nose for basically insinuating that I'm such a piece of shit that I'd blackmail Jocelyn to get her to marry me."

Luke knew he was being stupid, considering he had, in fact, used leverage to get Jocelyn to say yes to his proposal. But it hurt all the same that Jack would suspect him of being so underhanded.

"I want to believe you. But until you can prove otherwise, I'm not giving you the benefit of the doubt," said Jack.

Luke raised his glass. "Cheers to that," he replied, sarcasm dripping from his voice.

CHAPTER THIRTEEN

It was close to ten p.m. when Jocelyn arrived home. Yawning, she listened for Luke and heard the shower running. Her stomach rumbled, but she was too exhausted to make anything.

As she stood staring dazedly at the inside of the fridge, she didn't hear Luke approach. When he touched her shoulder, she jumped.

"Whoa there," he said. "What are you doing?"

"I don't know. I'm hungry, but making anything right now is beyond me."

Luke gently pushed her aside. "I'll make you something."

Jocelyn wanted to protest, but she didn't have the energy. She sat at the bar and watched Luke collect ingredients.

"Grilled cheese?" she guessed as he began to butter some bread.

"My specialty. Prepare to be amazed."

She nearly started telling him how she made grilled

cheese—mayo instead of butter, plus salting the pan for an extra kick—but she bit her tongue. When he began taking off the plastic on the American cheese, though, she nearly bit her tongue in half.

"You look like you're in pain," he said as he placed the bread in the heated skillet.

"I am."

Luke just laughed. "I promise you'll love it. If not, you can divorce me."

"Even I'm not petty enough to divorce someone over a sandwich."

"Oh, I doubt that, Miss Fancy Chef."

When he finally placed the finished product in front of her, she made herself take a bite before she could overthink things. To her surprise, the sandwich was good. Amazing? No, not amazing, but just what she needed after a long day at work.

She ate the grilled cheese in record time. Luke watched her, a smile on his face.

It was in that moment that Jocelyn realized that they were alone together. Sure, she'd moved in a week ago, but she'd barely been at his apartment. *Their* apartment.

It was sparsely furnished, with zero pictures on the walls. Luke kept it clean, probably because he wasn't here much. Like a lot of bachelors, Luke's place included only the essentials: an oversized couch, a giant TV, and a microwave.

He hadn't even had a trashcan for the bathroom, and he'd owned all of one bath towel. Jocelyn had been glad she'd been able to make the place slightly more habitable.

She had been worried the two of them would have too much stuff, but Luke apparently preferred to live simply.

Jocelyn cleared her throat. "Thank you for dinner. I'm going to take a shower and go to bed."

Before she got up, though, her phone chimed. When she saw that it was Bekah texting her, Jocelyn grimaced. Her best friend was still not happy with her, although she'd promised she'd try to be understanding. *Try* being the operative word.

"What's that face for?" asked Luke.

"Oh, it's nothing. I told Bekah about us getting married, and she wasn't happy about it."

"Ah. I'm sorry. That seems to be a theme lately."

"Was somebody pissed at you?"

Luke scowled. "Jack told me he'd break my kneecaps if I hurt you."

Jocelyn gaped at Luke. Jack had said that? Although she considered him a friend, they weren't exactly close, either. She'd had no idea Jack would want to protect her.

Then again, she was friends with Gwen, and Jack was extremely protective of his fiancée.

"Everyone is mad at me." Jocelyn sighed. "Gwen, Bekah, my sister. My dad will barely speak to me. People are acting like we deliberately ran over a bunch of puppies. You'd think one of them would just be happy for us."

"Maybe none of them believe us when we tell them why."

That statement made Jocelyn's stomach twist. She'd tried her best to sound as effusive as possible, but she wasn't a great actress, either. Did everyone think she was full of crap? The thought was humiliating. Even worse was the idea that no one could believe that Luke Wright of all people would want to marry her in the first place.

"They'll get over it," said Luke, breaking through her self-pitying thoughts. "I think they're just upset they weren't a part of the wedding. It's a big thing, getting married without telling anyone."

Jocelyn didn't know why, but she wanted to spill her guts to Luke. Maybe it was the quiet of the apartment or the way he was looking at her. But she felt like she could trust him. It was a dangerous feeling. She'd trusted him once before, and that had ended disastrously.

"I thought my dad would be supportive, at least. He's always worried that I'd end up alone. He'd tell me that I couldn't give up on finding somebody." Jocelyn smiled sadly. "He'd tell me stories about how he'd fallen in love with my mom. Then again, considering she ran off without a second thought, it wasn't a great love story at the end of the day."

"I've never heard you talk about your mom."

Jocelyn bit her lip. "There's not much to say. She left when I was ten."

"You haven't talked to her since?"

"No. I don't know where she is. She could be dead." At his shocked look, she added, "I know that sounds cold. But it's like talking about a stranger, you know?"

"You haven't wanted to find her?"

"Oh, I thought about it when I was younger. I'd write letters to her, even though I didn't know where she lived. I'd dream about the day she'd return and tell us she'd decided to come back. When you're a kid, you'll forgive anything, I guess. But by the time I was a teenager, I knew if I saw her again, I'd just rage at her." Jocelyn shrugged a shoulder. "What's the point? She left, I grew up, it's over."

Luke didn't look convinced. Jocelyn was used to that look on people's faces. They always wanted her to confess that she missed her mom, that she wanted a relationship with her after everything. But Jocelyn wasn't lying to herself: she wanted nothing to do with the woman who'd abandon her two young daughters without a second thought.

Jocelyn rubbed the back of her neck, suddenly self-conscious. "I guess grilled cheese makes me want to talk about fun subjects," she tried to say lightly.

But Luke didn't laugh. He was staring at his hands. "My parents are hardly going to win best parents of the year, either," he said. He clenched his fists. "They were good to me, I guess. But not to my brother."

"I've always wondered what happened to him."

Luke was still looking at his hands. Then he smiled at her, and he seemed to shrug the heaviness right off his shoulders. "I'm tired. Let's go to bed."

Jocelyn blushed, but Luke added, "Alone."

That just made her blush harder, because she was an idiot and it felt like a rejection. She turned on her heel so she wouldn't make a bigger fool of herself in front of her husband. Her husband who seemed okay with separate bedrooms now.

She brushed her teeth with jerky movements, reminding herself that this was just a temporary arrangement. None of this was real. So what if Luke was being kind to her tonight?

She knew that could change overnight. He'd done the same thing in high school. Yes, people changed, but not in the major aspects of their personalities. If he could dump her without so much as a single regret as a teenager, what coldness did the adult version of him possess deep inside?

Jocelyn went to her room and shut the door, locking it for good measure. She let Fluffer out of his cage. The rabbit stretched and hopped around, but he mostly just wanted to be picked up. He'd sit at Jocelyn's feet and wiggle his nose when he wanted to be petted.

Jocelyn obliged, stroking Fluffer's silky ears. He closed his eyes in contentment. "At least you still like me," she murmured.

That feeling that felt like a black hole opening up inside her gut threatened to overwhelm her. She sat down on her bed. She hated feeling sorry for herself, but she'd also never experienced having both her dad and her sister being upset with her at the same time. Usually it was just Alex, with their dad wanting them to make up and be sisters.

There was a knock on her door. "Jocelyn? Are you still awake?"

She considered ignoring Luke's call but sighed and opened the door, Fluffer still in her arms.

"Oh, sorry." Luke looked nonplussed. "I didn't know rabbits liked to cuddle."

He seemed so surprised that Jocelyn couldn't help but chuckle. "Some do. What, did you think I just kept him in his cage all day and night?"

Luke shrugged. "Yes?"

She held Fluffer out to Luke, the rabbit barely opening his eyes at the movement. "Come on, hold him. He won't bite. Well, probably. Don't get your fingers too close to his mouth or else he'll think they're carrots."

Luke took the rabbit awkwardly, like she was handing him a bomb instead of an animal. Fluffer's eyes widened, and Jocelyn could tell that Luke's tension was making the rabbit tense, too.

"Loosen up," she instructed. "He can tell you're not feeling this."

"I never asked to hold him!"

At that, Fluffer began to wiggle to get down. Jocelyn took him and set him on the floor before he could start bunny kicking. His giant feet could pack a serious punch when he wanted to.

Annoyed now, Fluffer hopped back to his cage and turned his back to the stupid humans who'd disturbed him for no reason.

"He doesn't seem like he's a fan of me," said Luke.

"Have you ever owned a pet?"

"My mom has always had little dogs, but I've never had anything that was mine. Tristan had a lizard when we were kids, but our mom got rid of it one day after it'd gotten out. He was devastated."

"How sad."

They both stared at Fluffer, watching him bathe himself. It was then that Jocelyn realized that she was only wearing a short nightgown. With Luke in his boxers and a t-shirt, she couldn't help but be reminded of the last time they hadn't been wearing much clothing.

"Did you need me for something?" asked Jocelyn, looking anywhere but at Luke right then.

"Um." Luke swallowed. "Did you need anything from the store tomorrow?"

It was such a banal question that it took Jocelyn a

moment to comprehend the question. It was also such a husbandly thing to ask about. She hated that her heart fluttered thinking about it.

"No, I'm okay," she stuttered.

"Okay, well, let me know if you think of anything."

Silence settled around them. Jocelyn waited for Luke to do anything—say anything. She waited for him to give in and kiss her. Considering the heat that was rising between them, she wondered at his self-restraint.

But then he shook his head and shut her door behind him without another word.

Scowling, Jocelyn threw one of her slippers at the door. Fluffer, used to these occasional outbursts, merely twitched an ear and continued bathing.

CHAPTER FOURTEEN

Luke didn't sleep. He couldn't stop thinking about how Jocelyn was just in the other room and how little she'd been wearing earlier. Every molecule in his body wanted to return to her room and make her his.

He groaned, punching down his pillow. But when sleep continued to elude him, he got up to go watch something on the TV in the living room.

But Jocelyn was already in there. She was asleep on the couch, the remote about to slip from her fingers onto the rug.

Luke tried to go back to his room, but he must've stepped on the one squeaky board in the apartment, because it alerted Jocelyn to his presence. Her eyes flew open at the same time that the remote hit the floor. She scrambled upward, soon getting tangled in the large blanket she'd wrapped herself in.

"It's just me," he said, helping her out of her predicament. "I didn't mean to startle you."

Jocelyn exhaled. "Crap, you scared me!"

"Why are you so jumpy?"

"I was dreaming about something. I think someone was chasing me." She shuddered.

Luke sat down next to her. Although he was tempted to take her into his arms, he refrained. Considering she'd rewrapped herself in the blanket, she didn't seem interested in a comforting hug.

"Sorry," he repeated. He gestured to the TV screen. "Couldn't sleep?"

"No. You either?"

"Nope."

They both watched the infomercial on the screen for a long moment, although the volume was so low that Luke couldn't even hear it.

"Why have the TV on with no sound?" he asked.

"It's the white noise. It puts me to sleep."

"Why not just put on a fan?"

"Because I like to watch something until I fall asleep." She wrinkled her nose at him. "Why all the questions?"

He didn't know. Or maybe he just wanted to keep her talking so he didn't do something stupid, like kiss her. Just sitting next to her, the scent of her filling his nose, was enough to make him wild.

He was glad it was dark, besides the TV, otherwise Jocelyn could see just how much, exactly, he wanted her. He grabbed another blanket to cover himself, though. Just in case.

Jocelyn eventually got up to get a glass of water. But as she sat down, she tripped over the remote still on the floor and spilled the water all over herself.

"Goddammit," she cursed. "It's all over the floor, too—"

Luke helped her up, checking her for any injuries. "Did you hurt yourself?"

"What? No, I'm fine. Just wet." She sighed. "Let me go get some paper towels—"

But Luke wasn't listening to her. He was gazing at her breasts that were basically bare now with her nightgown soaked. The memory of kissing and sucking on her breasts two weeks ago rose inside his mind. To his delight, her nipples beaded, as if reacting to his thoughts.

"Luke," she whispered. "The water."

He turned off the TV. Then he pulled her into his arms.

"Fuck the water," he muttered before kissing her.

Jocelyn gasped in surprise, and then she gasped more loudly when he lifted her into his arms and carried her to his bedroom. At first he'd considered taking her to her room, but he didn't want an audience of one judgmental rabbit.

"Luke," she said again. "What are you—?"

He stopped. He could just make out her eyes in the dim hallway. "You have two choices: I return you to the room and you lock your door. Or I take you to mine and we finally give in to thing between us."

She took in a shuddering breath. Luke waited, his heart pounding in his chest.

"Your room," she finally whispered.

"Thank God."

He strode into his bedroom and lay her on the bed, nearly ripping her wet nightgown off of her. Then he was on top of her and kissing her like a man starved. She gave as good as she got. She ran her hands down his back and lifted his shirt up to his waist.

He tossed his own shirt aside. Jocelyn caressed his chest, even going so far as to dip her fingers in the waistband of his boxers. His entire body shuddered at the brief contact. His cock was hard and pulsing already. It wouldn't take much to finish him off.

Luke gently pushed her hands away before kissing down her body. He pushed the panel of her panties aside, and he found her damp already. As he licked through her folds, she called out his name, her hands gripping his hair.

He played with her until she was writhing, desperate for her release. But he wanted to feel her explode around him. After one last kiss, Luke rose and went to his nightstand to grab a condom.

"Tell me you want this," he growled after he'd sheathed himself in the latex. He pushed Jocelyn's legs further apart and pushed just the tip inside her sheath. "Say it, baby."

Her eyes were wide in the dark. Her breaths came in pants. When she didn't immediately answer, Luke pulled out, teasing her instead.

Jocelyn gripped his biceps. "Are you going to make me beg?"

"Of course I am. You need to learn how to beg some-times, dearest wife."

Her nails dug into his skin, but he just laughed wickedly. He kissed her mouth, just teasing touches, while his cock simply slipped through her slick folds. She arched, trying to press him inside, but he wouldn't let her.

"God, Luke, you asshole!" She nipped at his bottom lip. "I want you. Fuck me already."

"Such a romantic." But then he pushed inside her, and they were both moaning in ecstasy.

Luke tried his best to keep things slow, to keep teasing Jocelyn, but his self-control wasn't limitless. Soon enough, he was thrusting harder and faster, Jocelyn egging him on.

His release burst upon him just moments after Jocelyn screamed and shook underneath him. He buried his face in her hair, gripping her hips to keep her still. Even as his orgasm was fading, Jocelyn arched and bucked, and he could feel a second orgasm follow her first one.

After Luke cleaned himself up and disposed of the condom, Jocelyn doing the same, he returned to bed to find his wife already having fallen asleep. Pulling her into an embrace, he inhaled the scent of her hair and fell asleep soon after.

IT WAS early morning when he felt Jocelyn stir. He pulled her closer to his body, mostly because he didn't want to wake up quite yet.

But Jocelyn wiggled out of his grasp. Soon, Luke could feel her looking at him.

He cracked open one eye. "Yes?"

Her expression was serious—too serious. "Why did you ice me out our senior year?"

Luke's sleepiness instantly vanished, but he shrugged a shoulder and closed his eyes. "Because I was a stupid teenager?" he muttered.

But he should've known Jocelyn wasn't going to let him out of this one. She began poking him, over and over, until he raised his arms in surrender. Flipping back to face her, he sighed.

It wasn't that he didn't want to tell her, or that he didn't feel like he owed her an explanation. But a big reason why had nothing to do with him—it was his brother's story. A story Tristan had forbidden Luke from telling anyone else.

But as Luke gazed at his wife, he knew he couldn't keep silent. He touched her cheek.

"I'm sorry," he said softly.

"Tell me why, then."

Luke sighed. Trying to order his thoughts, he began haltingly, not wanting to reveal too many things regarding Tristan.

He'd never talked about this, he realized. No one had known, and Luke had always figured it had been better that way.

"You know my younger brother, Tristan," he said into the dark, gazing at the ceiling now.

"I knew who he was, but I didn't ever hang out with him."

"He was always the black sheep of the family. He was the artist, the rebel. He didn't want to do anything our parents wanted him to do. They would enroll him in different sports, but he'd refuse to attend practices. He also got bad grades in school. I remember my dad yelling at Tristan when he'd failed some science class when he was in middle school."

Luke told Jocelyn of how, when he'd been younger, he'd simply done the opposite of his brother and had been grateful that he didn't get yelled at.

Luke found school easy; he aced tests with little study-ing, whereas Tristan, no matter how many hours he studied, would struggle. Their dad soon felt that Tristan was failing school simply to rebel. Considering Tristan eventually gave up studying altogether, their dad hadn't been completely wrong.

"As we got older, Tristan withdrew. He wouldn't come down to dinner. He would refuse to go to family events, no matter how much my dad threatened or my mom begged. He lived in his room, basically. So when we found out that he was dating a girl, we were all kind of shocked."

"Why would that be shocking?" asked Jocelyn.

Luke took her hand, smiling sadly. "Tristan was such a recluse that my parents assumed he had zero friends. I never saw him with anyone at school, either. So to hear he was dating someone at all was a surprise."

"But my parents were furious. The girl was from a 'bad' family." Luke rolled his eyes. "I told them they should leave off, but my dad went on a rampage. And when Tristan ran off with her one weekend, that was the beginning of the end."

A few days later, the police returned Tristan to their parents, the girl to hers. Gregory was so enraged at the humiliation of his younger son being arrested that he'd quickly packed Tristan off to a boarding school in the middle of nowhere Utah.

Even worse, his parents turned the girl's family into pariahs on the island. They lost their business and their reputations.

"When I saw what my dad was capable of," continued Luke, "I knew I had to end things with you. He never would've approved of our relationship. He would've torpedoed your family just like he had Mina's."

Jocelyn's eyes widened. "Mina North? That was who

your brother had dated? I always wondered what had happened to her. Alex was friends with her, but then she just…disappeared. Alex was devastated."

"Yeah, and it was because of my fucking parents." Luke sat up now. "I didn't know what else to do but to treat you like dirt. I knew if I told you what was going on, you'd tell me that it didn't matter, to stand up to my parents, but I knew what would've happened. I couldn't watch that happen."

Jocelyn was silent for a long moment. Then she sat up and leaned against him. Luke let out a breath he hadn't even noticed he'd been holding.

"For all of these years, you let me keep on hating you," she whispered. "Why?"

"What was the point? I hurt you. Your anger was justified."

"But you did it to protect me." She sighed. "Even if it was a stupid thing to do. It was, by the way. You should've just told me."

Exasperated, Luke snapped, "That's exactly why I didn't. Because you would've gone straight to my dad and told him to eat shit."

That made Jocelyn chuckle. "Probably." Then, she said, "I'm surprised he was okay with you marrying me now."

"When there's money on the line, my dad is fine with bending the rules." Luke snorted.

Luke held Jocelyn close, feeling the tension in his body melt away to some degree. But whenever he thought about Tristan and the hell he'd gone through, his stomach twisted. He hadn't told Jocelyn the half of it. But that would be Tristan's story to tell, not Luke's.

"Does this mean you don't hate me anymore?" said Luke quietly.

"I don't know." But Luke could feel her smiling. "I'm still annoyed that you thought you could make such a decision for me. That was a shitty thing to do."

"I'll take that as a yes," he replied before kissing her forehead.

CHAPTER FIFTEEN

Despite their strange beginnings, married life fell into a normal routine. Jocelyn went to work while Luke stayed home to work in his office. He'd tell her goodbye and sometimes even have coffee ready for her to take with her. She'd been tempted to remind him that the restaurant had plenty of coffee available—and better coffee, too—but she hadn't had the heart.

They spent most of their nights together as well. Jocelyn had unofficially moved into Luke's bedroom, although she hadn't moved her things into his closet. Although they were married, that step seemed too large for Jocelyn. Besides, she'd figured, the closet was small. It'd be better for them both if she kept her things in a separate room.

Fluffer became acquainted with his new home quickly. He was shy of Luke, but after a few evenings of Luke giving Fluffer his favorite veggies, the rabbit came around and let Luke pet him on occasion. He was still Jocelyn's rabbit, though, a fact which she appreciated. If this marriage failed, at least she'd still have her beloved rabbit to keep her company.

Jocelyn knew that this routine of theirs wouldn't last. Real life would rear its ugly head soon enough. They'd both been avoiding their families—at least as much as you could on a small island—and the peace and quiet they'd been enjoying was simply an illusion.

Alex occasionally texted Jocelyn about their dad, but otherwise she'd been distant. Their dad completely ignored any talk of Jocelyn's marriage. Whenever Jocelyn mentioned Luke, Pete's expression would close off. It got to a point that Jocelyn simply acted like she didn't have a husband at all whenever she had to go over to her dad's place.

She and Alex, with financial help from Luke, had chosen a day nurse to assist their dad as needed. Pete had balked at first, but Jocelyn had been happy to see him accept the change. Nora was a no-nonsense nurse who never seemed to stop moving. She'd come into the house like a whirlwind, and she was so frank that Jocelyn had been amused to see her dad cowed into submission.

A month had passed since Jocelyn and Luke had married, which meant that they'd have to meet with Opal very soon. Jocelyn dreaded the meeting, while Luke took it simply as another hoop to jump through.

When they arrived at Opal's home, a large Victorian on the north side of the island, Jocelyn wished she'd worn something dressier. A strange woman Jocelyn didn't recognize opened the door for them and said something about going to get Opal.

The house screamed opulence, and entering the grand

hallway, Jocelyn felt like they'd been hurtled back in time a century ago. Although the house was tiny compared to the Wright mansion, it was clearly well-maintained. It was a jewel of a place that was probably worth millions despite the lack of square footage.

Jocelyn wiped her sweaty palms on her pants. She'd worn her hair down, which she regretted, because it made her feel even more self-conscious that she was sweating with nerves.

"Are you okay?" Luke shot her a look.

"I'll survive."

He didn't seem convinced, but he didn't have time to probe more deeply. Opal came down the stairs. Wearing a mink coat and diamond earrings, she somehow managed not to seem out of place despite the occasion.

Jocelyn barely stopped herself from curtseying. This woman wasn't the queen! Yet Opal held herself like she was, and Jocelyn shook her hand with an awestruck expression.

"Let's get this over with," said Opal, motioning to the pair. "I have an engagement this evening."

"What, is she going to set sail on the *Titanic?*" whispered Jocelyn to Luke.

Luke snorted, which made Opal turn her head to look at them with a suspicious expression. Clearly, Opal wouldn't appreciate any jokes on her behalf.

Opal took them to her living room—no, sitting room. Parlor? Jocelyn didn't know what to call it. It was filled with artwork on the walls, vases on every surface, and sculptures probably worth more than Jocelyn made in a year. A grand piano sat in one corner, freshly waxed and dusted.

"Do you play?" asked Jocelyn, gesturing to the instrument.

Opal sniffed. "Never wanted to learn."

Jocelyn decided she'd keep her mouth shut unless it was absolutely necessary for her to speak.

Opal assessed them with her eagle-eyed gaze for what felt like an eternity. Jocelyn forced herself not to squirm or wipe her sweaty palms a second time on her pants. Or worse, on the heavily embroidered sofa that they were sitting on.

"So," said Opal. She reached into a small chest on the table in front of her and pulled out a cigarette. She gestured vaguely at them both. "Smoke?"

Both Jocelyn and Luke declined. Jocelyn barely smothered a cough when Opal blew a cloud of smoke her way. It made Jocelyn's eyes water.

"Esther, you know, was my greatest friend. She was the only woman I ever gave a damn about. Most women, you know, are such useless ninnies. You'd criticize one of them, and they'd burst into tears. But not Esther. She gave as good as she got. I'll admit, I wasn't pleased when she married Walter, but he was a decent sort of fellow. And he didn't mind following Esther's lead."

Opal exhaled another cloud of smoke. "Shame about her son, though. Yes, your father." She looked at Luke. "A complete disappointment. I'm sure you can't disagree, either. Don't scowl at me. You know I'm right. A petty, self-righteous windbag. Esther indulged him too much when he was a child, and now everyone is paying for it."

Jocelyn glanced at Luke. His expression was calm, although she could just make out a tic in his jaw.

"At any rate, here we are. Esther was always full of ridiculous schemes. I told her not to involve me anymore, but she had to have the last laugh before we buried her six feet under." Opal sighed. "She wanted me to make sure you married a woman you loved." That made the older woman snort. "The ironic thing being that I myself don't much believe in romantic love."

Jocelyn caught Luke's gaze. "Then why do this?" asked Jocelyn.

"Because Esther asked me to. Simple as that. Oh, don't look so upset. I'm not going to mess everything up for my own amusement. Esther's ghost would haunt me if I tried." Opal stubbed out her cigarette. "I can't say I'm particularly impressed at the moment. You both sit there like you haven't so much as held hands, let alone made love."

Luke coughed, while Jocelyn blushed. Did they need to provide proof they'd slept together? Jocelyn was mortified.

"I thought this was about love," Luke ground out.

Opal chuckled. "It is. Sex is a huge part of that. Now you're both embarrassed. I thought young people nowadays didn't mind being explicit."

Jocelyn snapped, "Not with random strangers old enough to be our grandmother."

Luke took Jocelyn's hand and squeezed it in warning. Jocelyn merely squeezed back, as if to say, *Don't tell me what to do.*

Opal, though, didn't seem offended. "Touché. What are your future plans? Where are you living? When will you have children?"

At the mention of children, Jocelyn let go of Luke's hand, a cold hand dancing down her spine.

Jocelyn had never been particularly interested in having children, mostly because that would mean putting her career on hold. She'd always figured that if she felt the urge one day, she'd figure out what she wanted to do.

But having a child with Luke? The thought made her mind whirl. Of course, it wouldn't happen. This marriage wasn't meant to last, and bringing a child into the equation would be the height of idiocy. Despite knowing that, Jocelyn's heart flipped, and she couldn't help but imagine a baby with his eyes and smile.

"We haven't discussed children," replied Luke blandly. "We've been busy with other things."

"That doesn't seem wise. What if one of you wants children and the other doesn't? That's not a thing you can compromise on," said Opal.

Luke glanced at Jocelyn out of the corner of his eye. "I would like children someday," he said slowly, "but considering Jocelyn would be the one literally carrying them, it'd be up to her when it would happen."

Jocelyn felt like she was being stripped bare in front of them both. She wished she could get up and leave. But she forced herself to smile and add, "I love my job too much to think about kids right now."

"How old are you?" said Opal.

"I'm only thirty."

"And in five years, you'll be thirty-five, and then you'll be too old for children. The clock's ticking. Don't delay until it's too late."

Before Jocelyn could retort, Luke replied, "I think we have plenty of time regardless. People aren't having kids in their twenties as much now."

"An ambitious woman," said Opal, "is a dangerous woman."

"You can't tell me you're not ambitious," countered Jocelyn.

"Of course. Which is why women like us are dangerous."

As the afternoon progressed, Opal continued to ask all sorts of questions, so many that Jocelyn soon lost track. She didn't know how Opal was keeping track; she wasn't exactly taking notes.

Luke was calm throughout, which Jocelyn found both impressive and annoying. She had to bite her tongue so many times she was surprised she hadn't already bitten the poor organ in half already.

"My last question and you can go," said Opal. Now she was looking squarely at Luke. "Do you love Jocelyn?"

Silence fell. Jocelyn waited for Luke's easy smile and the lie tripping from his mouth with ease.

But the words didn't come. He cleared his throat, took Jocelyn's hand, and said to Opal, "What is love, anyway?"

Jocelyn stared, shocked. Opal just raised a penciled eyebrow and said nothing in reply.

JOCELYN WAS silent as they drove home. Luke seemed tense, his shoulders hunched. He opened his mouth more than once, but then he just shook his head.

Jocelyn was torn between feeling hurt and being angry that Luke hadn't lied. Wasn't the entire point of this thing to lie? Why would he blow their chances like this?

And why did it hurt so much that he hadn't been able to say the words in the first place?

Wouldn't you rather he be honest? her mind whispered.

She was afraid to admit that she didn't know the answer to that question.

"You're quiet," said Luke.

"Because I don't know what to say to you."

"I know I messed up back there—"

"Do you actually want this inheritance of yours? Because giving an answer like that to Opal seems like the best way to torpedo this entire thing."

Luke's hands clenched on the steering wheel. "I'm aware of this. I fucked up. You don't have to rub it in."

"I'm not rubbing it in. I'm trying to understand why you did it."

"I don't fucking know!" he burst out.

Jocelyn reared backward. He'd never yelled at her like this. It stung, almost as much as his vague, dismissive answer about loving her.

"I realize I'm not the woman you would've married or one you'd fall in love with," she said roughly, "but the least you could do is uphold your end of the bargain."

As Jocelyn went to her room, Luke to his, she reminded herself that she couldn't let herself feel hurt when Luke rejected her. He wasn't a real husband. It didn't matter how good the sex was.

"I should never have had sex with him," she whispered to herself. "I knew that, but I kept doing it anyway."

Fluffer nudged at her foot, reminding her that it was his dinnertime. When he nipped at her ankle, though, she knew she couldn't ignore him any longer.

"You'll always bring me back down to earth, won't you?" she said to the rabbit.

Fluffer kicked his back feet and hopped to the kitchen to remind Jocelyn where his food was.

LATER THAT EVENING, Jocelyn received a text from Alex, asking her if she'd heard from their dad. Jocelyn hadn't, and when she called his phone, he didn't pick up.

Luke was still in his bedroom. After returning Fluffer to his cage, she stood at Luke's door, wondering if she should tell him where she was going. But then she decided against it.

She didn't feel like seeing her husband right then, anyway.

She rushed to her dad's, telling herself that more than likely he'd turned his phone off without realizing it. When she stepped inside the house, she had to turn on a light, it was so dark.

"Dad?" Jocelyn called. "Dad?" she repeated more loudly.

Then to her relief, she heard him reply, "In my bedroom!"

She found him in bed. Considering it was only six p.m., it was extremely early for him to be in bed.

"Are you sick?" said Jocelyn, concerned. "Why are you in bed?"

"Because I wanted to finish my book in here." He gave her a look that told her she was overreacting.

She still felt his forehead anyway, but he wasn't feverish. He soon batted her hands away, annoyance on his face.

"Why didn't you pick up your phone?" she asked. She looked around. "Where is it, anyway?"

He shrugged. "Don't know."

They eventually found it wedged in between couch cushions. It was on, but it was on vibrate. Jocelyn plugged it in on her dad's nightstand and made sure the ring was on—and that it would ring loudly.

"You have to pick up your phone. I've told you that a million times. Alex was so worried she had me come to check on you," said Jocelyn.

Pete sighed and closed his book. "I'm fine. I'm not a child."

"Of course not, but—"

"No buts." He rubbed his forehead and then sighed a second time. "Jossy, you do too much. You've always done too much."

"I know I'm bossy and overbearing—"

"Yeah, you are, but that's not what I mean." He took her hand, and he touched the wedding band on her left hand. "Why did you marry Luke Wright? Tell me."

Jocelyn tried to take her hand back, but her dad wouldn't let her go. Her heart pounded in her ears.

"I love him," she whispered.

"He has money."

"So?"

"I know you. I know you wouldn't marry any guy out of the blue. You aren't your sister." Pete chuckled. "Her showing up one day, married to a stranger? Nobody would be surprised. But you? You aren't impulsive. So there has to be a good reason why you did this, and not because your feelings got away from you."

Jocelyn couldn't speak. She wanted to tell her dad everything, but the words died in her throat. Mostly, she felt ashamed—ashamed that she'd been so desperate that she'd married a man for his money.

"I'm sorry for how I've been the last month." Her dad's eyes filled with tears. "I couldn't bear the thought that you did this for me. Oh, I know you know about the mortgage, the medical bills. You're too smart for your own good. And you always think you can shoulder any burden."

He pinched her chin. "I'm sorry I wasn't home with you two enough. I should've done better by you girls."

Now Jocelyn was crying. "You did your best. I know you did."

"But it wasn't good enough." His smile was so sad that it tore Jocelyn's heart in two.

He opened his arms, and Jocelyn let herself be comforted. She couldn't remember the last time she'd let herself cry in her dad's arms. Probably not since her mom had left them all behind.

"I don't know what I'm going to do," she murmured.

"No matter what you decide," said Pete solemnly, "know that you're not alone. Okay? Promise me you know that."

Jocelyn assured him that she did. But even as she said the words, she knew they were a lie. She had to figure this out for herself; nobody could save her from her own mistakes.

CHAPTER SIXTEEN

When Luke saw the unknown number come up on his phone, he nearly let it go to voicemail. But something about it piqued his interest. Answering on the last ring, he expected to hear a voice he didn't recognize.

"Hey, bro," said his younger brother, Tristan.

Luke nearly dropped his phone. "Tristan?"

"Yeah. It's me."

Luke got up from his office chair, glad that he was alone in the apartment right then. He didn't need Jocelyn asking him why he was pacing around the apartment. Which he was definitely already doing.

"It's been a while," said Luke.

"How long has it been? I've lost track."

Although Luke had recognized his brother's voice, Tristan still sounded different. Then again, it'd been a good ten years since they'd spoken.

"Where are you right now?" said Luke.

"Oh, here and there. It doesn't matter."

"I think our parents would disagree."

Luke cursed himself, half-expecting Tristan to hang up right then and there. Tristan hated their parents with a deep, burning passion. Luke couldn't blame him, even if he wished Tristan would try to patch things up with them.

"I wanted to wish you congratulations. I heard the news," said Tristan. "Although I'm offended you didn't invite me."

"How could I invite you when I don't even know where the fuck you live?"

Tristan chuckled. "You would've figured something out. How's married life?"

Luke didn't know how to respond to that question. He couldn't believe his brother, who'd avoided speaking with him for so long, had suddenly wanted to call and chat.

"Jocelyn and I are adapting."

"Adapting? Well, I guess it makes sense, considering why you married her in the first place."

Luke stared out the apartment window, watching as a mom with a young child was doing her best to get the little one back into her stroller. The toddler was not having it, however, and threw herself down onto the sidewalk, kicking and screaming.

Luke rather wanted to kick and scream himself. Or reach through the phone and strangle his brother.

"What is this all about?" said Luke, irritation lacing his voice. "Clearly you're keeping tabs on us, so you still give a shit about the family."

"Only the smallest bit of shit."

"Enough that you know that I got married."

"Don't flatter yourself. I didn't stalk you on social media. Granny Esther's lawyer found me and contacted me about my inheritance. He also told me about yours. Sounds like you're getting almost all of the money. Congrats on that one, too."

The toddler outside was now trying to run in the other direction. Her poor mom visibly sighed and went after her daughter, picking up the screaming child and carrying her like a sack of potatoes over her shoulder.

"I don't blame you for getting married to get your inheritance," said Tristan. "But then again, I never understood why you always went along with what the family wanted. You've always been the golden child."

"I'm doing this for myself. Not for our parents."

"I doubt that. Do you really expect me to believe Dad didn't guilt-trip you? That Mom didn't beg you to make sure she didn't end up on the streets?" Tristan snorted. "When in reality they'd just have to downsize, sell off some expensive artwork, and live in a normal-sized house. Oh, the inhumanity."

"What do you want, Tristan?" asked Luke, tired now.

"Nothing. I've never wanted a damn thing from this family. But this lawyer tells me the only way I can get my money is to come back to Hazel Island and make nice."

"And you want me to do what, exactly? Sounds like that's entirely your problem."

"I want you to tell the parents that I'll come, but I won't say when. I also won't come unless they keep their mouths shut."

The mom with the toddler had placed the little girl in her stroller finally and had walked off. But not before the toddler had started laughing hysterically.

Luke marveled at how quickly kids' moods could

change. They could forget in an instant that they'd even been unhappy. He wished it was that easy when you were an adult.

"Are you listening to what I'm saying?" said Tristan.

Luke rolled his eyes. "I'm not going to be your go-between. If you want to say something to our parents, that's on you. I know you're still angry about the past—"

"You don't know. Don't fucking talk to me about the past."

"Fine. I don't know. You never told me. But that's on you, too. If you want to waste your life running around the world because you refuse to face your own demons, that's your choice. But don't drag me into it."

Luke thought for a moment that his brother had hung up. Then, Tristan asked, "Do you love her?"

Luke didn't have to ask who he meant. "I wouldn't marry someone I didn't love."

"That's not an answer. You know she probably married you just for your money, right? Maybe for once, the great Luke Wright won't get everything he wants."

"You sound bitter. Have you ever tried therapy?"

Tristan did hang up after that. Luke stared at his phone, wondering what the hell had just happened.

Had Tristan just called to fight? Luke didn't understand it. He also didn't fully understand why his brother couldn't just move on, either. He was still stuck on how their parents had treated him when they'd been teenagers. It'd been over ten years, for God's sake.

Tristan's words, though, were insidious enough to creep under Luke's skin. It didn't help that Jocelyn had been frosty with him since their meeting with Opal that weekend. Luke knew he'd hurt her feelings, but he didn't understand why she'd been so upset.

He wasn't in love with her, just like she wasn't in love with him. They were doing this for his inheritance. They'd both been well aware of the stakes when they'd married.

Sounds like you care a little too much about your wife's feelings, a voice whispered.

He cared about Jocelyn. He'd allow that. She was a friend—and now a friend with benefits.

That didn't mean Luke was falling for her. He wouldn't let his feelings get to that point, anyway. Unlike his brother, he refused to let himself be irrational and emotional.

Even as Luke told himself that, he thought of how he'd woken up just that morning alone in his bed. He'd missed rolling over to see Jocelyn sleeping next to him in the last few days or reaching over for her and feeling her snuggle against him.

You're just horny. Don't confuse love for needing some sex.

Maybe that was it: he was just feeling rejected. Yet at the thought of going elsewhere for sex, his stomach twisted. He might not be married for love, but he couldn't cheat on his wife, either.

"Don't get distracted," he reminded himself. Because he knew if he lost focus, the consequences would be disastrous.

WHEN JOCELYN ARRIVED HOME, Luke was in the living room watching TV. She didn't say anything as she walked past him. Clearly, she was still pissed with him.

Luke followed her. He watched as she let Fluffer out of

his cage. The rabbit stretched and hopped toward Luke, wiggling his fluffy tail in greeting.

Jocelyn watched Luke pet Fluffer with narrowed eyes. "He seems to really like you."

"I might've been bribing him while you were at work."

"So that's where all of the apples have gone."

Luke scratched Fluffer on his head; the rabbit's eyes began to close in ecstasy. But soon enough, the rabbit returned to his first love and hopped into Jocelyn's lap.

"Why did you get a rabbit? Most people get a dog or a cat," said Luke, leaning against the doorframe.

"I'm allergic to dogs and cats. I always wanted a pet growing up, but we never had the money. Alex brought home a rabbit one day, though. We still don't know where she got it."

Luke's lips twitched. "Why do I get the feeling she caught a wild rabbit to bring home?"

"It wasn't wild, thankfully. I think a friend of hers gave it to her. She was only seven at the time, and apparently her friend's rabbit had had babies and needed to get rid of them…" Jocelyn shrugged. "Anyway, the end of this story is that we had to give the rabbit away when my dad found out we'd been hiding it in the closet for a week."

"It took him a whole week?"

"It helps that rabbits are so quiet."

Fluffer's eyes were closed now, although occasionally he'd twitch in his sleep.

"After that, I knew I wanted to get a rabbit of my own when I was grown up," said Jocelyn. A smile played about her face. "It took a second for that to happen. And despite their reputation, rabbits make good pets."

"My headphone cord would beg to differ."

Jocelyn laughed. "Oh no, I'm so sorry. He loves cords. I'll replace your headphones."

Luke waved a hand. "It's fine. It was my fault for leaving them out where he could get them."

Luke watched as Jocelyn petted and even kissed Fluffer. Seeing her like this, gentle and tender with her rabbit, made Luke feel jealous.

Yes, he was jealous of a rabbit. *You're an idiot*, he told himself.

"I wouldn't have taken you for an animal person," said Luke.

"Why is that?"

He shrugged. "You just aren't…warm and fuzzy, I guess."

That made Jocelyn shoot him a wry look. "I might be a bitch to humans, but I'm nice to animals. And even small children. Despite what you might think, I'm not a goblin twenty-four seven."

"I never thought of you as a goblin. Just prickly."

Wrinkling her nose, she got up after Fluffer hopped away, already done with his short nap.

Before she could leave, Luke said, "I'm sorry for what I said at Opal's. It was a stupid answer."

Jocelyn wouldn't look at him now. "You were just being honest. But you should be more careful. We don't want to put getting your inheritance in jeopardy." Despite her words, her voice sounded hollow.

"It's not just about the money," he snapped.

"It isn't?"

They gazed at each other, the moment lengthening.

Luke didn't know how to explain. The money was important, but now it seemed like such a stupid excuse.

He reached out and touched her cheek. "I've missed you," he admitted.

"I'm right here."

He stepped closer. "I've missed you in my bed."

He waited, hoping against hope that she wouldn't push him away. When she kissed him, his chest tightened while the rest of his body was ignited.

He only broke the kiss when he felt a creature on his foot, a creature that was now nibbling on his shoelaces.

"Your rabbit is a cock-block," he muttered.

Jocelyn laughed heartily. "He's just defending my virtue. What a good bunny you are," she cooed at Fluffer.

As Luke watched his wife walk away, her ass swaying, he said to Fluffer in a low voice, "You might've won the battle, but I'll win this war."

CHAPTER SEVENTEEN

Jocelyn awoke to the smell of bacon and the sound of Luke swearing. Opening her eyes, she had a moment of panic when she looked at the clock, but then she remembered it was her day off.

When she heard more swearing, she put on her robe and hurried to the kitchen.

Smoke was emanating from a skillet on the stove. Luke was desperately waving it away with a kitchen towel, but he wasn't quick enough. The smoke detector began to scream in protest.

Jocelyn stifled a laugh and helped him wave away the smoke. The detector finally shut off after a few more seconds of painful screeching.

"Good morning?" said Jocelyn. She took in the state of the kitchen. Bowls and utensils were everywhere. There were multiple pots and pans on the stove, and there was some kind of batter splattered on the countertops.

She made sure the burner under the smoking bacon was

off. Fortunately, the bacon itself looked okay. Nothing was a greater tragedy than bacon burnt to a crisp.

Luke grimaced at her. "I wanted to surprise you."

"Well, you definitely did that."

A timer went off, and he gently moved her aside to take out a pan from the oven. Jocelyn wasn't entirely sure what the concoction was supposed to be. Cinnamon rolls? No, maybe it was a frittata. She honestly couldn't tell.

"Do you need help?" Her voice was uncharacteristically gentle.

Luke glared at her. "Don't pity me. No, I don't need your help. I want to do this for you."

"Please don't burn down the apartment, though."

"I won't." He smacked her ass with a towel. "Now get out before I throw you out."

Jocelyn did as she was told, although it was one of the hardest things she'd ever had to do. Listening to Luke clatter around in the kitchen, clearly not having any idea what he was doing, was painful. If she could just show him how to use the mixer, or that he shouldn't turn the burners on to their highest setting unless he really did want to set the apartment on fire…

Somehow, Luke managed to finish breakfast. Jocelyn was presented with bacon, some kind of pastry, and very runny scrambled eggs.

Luke watched her intently as she took her first bite of eggs. She didn't mind wet scrambled eggs, but these were nearly raw. And they had some kind of spice in them that made her wince. Something strange, like cloves or nutmeg.

"Well?" Luke leaned forward.

Jocelyn took another bite, just in case that first one was

just a one-off. But no, the next one was even worse. Added to the nutmeg flavor was one of intense salt. So much salt that it tasted sour. She grabbed her glass of orange juice and instantly regretted the choice. All of those flavors together made her gag.

"Oh God," she said, feeling terrible, "I'm so sorry. It's not that bad, I swear. It was just the orange juice with it all—"

Luke took her fork and ate a bite of eggs. He chewed, then chewed some more. And then he turned to the sink and spat out the eggs. After turning on the garbage disposal, he gave Jocelyn a wry look.

"Those are fucking terrible. No, Christ, don't keep eating them. I don't want to have to take you to the hospital."

"What in the world did you put in them?"

He shrugged. "Honestly? I can't even remember. I just kept adding different things in the hopes that it'd work out."

Jocelyn poked at the roll on her plate. "What is in this one?"

Luke grabbed the roll and took a bite. At least this time, he swallowed. "I mean, it's not good, but it's not inedible."

Jocelyn agreed with that assessment: it had zero flavor and was dry as a bone. But it didn't make her gag.

Fortunately, the bacon was decent. She ate the strips with relish, her stomach still rumbling afterward, though.

"I wanted to surprise you," said Luke. He rubbed the back of his neck. "I thought it'd be easy. Guess not."

He looked so abashed that Jocelyn barely restrained the urge to kiss him. "I can't remember the last time someone cooked for me," she admitted. "I'm usually the one doing that."

"Really? Nobody?"

"No, not that I can remember. The cooking has always been on me." She smiled grimly. "That's probably why I tend to eat trash when it's just me. I shouldn't tell you this, but I eat Hot Pockets way too often for a chef."

He winked at her. "Your secret is safe with me."

Jocelyn went around to the other side of the counter, feeling out of sorts. Her heart was doing that annoying flip-flop thing inside her chest.

Most of all, she was annoyed that Luke kept trying to be nice to her. It was easier when he made her angry. When she was angry, she could avoid him.

But when he treated her like somebody who deserved to be taken care of, she was like a moth to a flame. She couldn't resist his orbit.

"Thank you." Her voice was soft. "It was very sweet of you to make me breakfast."

Now he looked embarrassed. "I didn't do it just to be sweet." He pulled her into an embrace. "I totally did it to get back on your good side." He slid his hand down to the small of her back before playing with the elastic of her pajama bottoms. "So? Is it working?"

"I admit nothing."

He leaned in and kissed the soft spot behind her ear. Jocelyn closed her eyes. When he pressed his mouth to hers, she couldn't help but give in.

The kiss was lazy and unhurried. He kissed her like they had all the time in the world. When she remembered that they didn't, a frisson of pain bloomed inside her.

"I should go take a shower," she said, her breath coming in quick puffs.

"Then I'll come with you."

And being human, Jocelyn couldn't find a reason to tell him no.

WHEN JOCELYN RECEIVED the first voicemail from an old chef colleague, she didn't think much of it. She'd forgotten about the voicemail entirely as she'd gotten swept up in work. Not only had she had to deal with multiple staff out sick, she had to contend with Kelly being mouthy and disrespectful.

Jocelyn took the girl aside after the dinner rush. She was pretty much at the point of wanting to fire her, but she also knew it would take way too long to find a replacement. Hazel Island wasn't brimming with sous chefs just waiting to fill the role.

Kelly didn't seem at all upset about being called into Jocelyn's office. The girl looked impatient, and she kept tapping her foot, as if she wanted to annoy Jocelyn as much as humanly possible.

But Jocelyn wasn't interested in Kelly's hollow promises. After warning her that if she didn't shape up and do her job, she'd be out on her ass, Kelly scowled and promised she'd try harder in the least convincing voice ever. But Jocelyn had to take her at her word.

So when she looked at her phone and was reminded that she had a voicemail waiting, she barely listened to it at first.

When she heard the words, "You'd be perfect for the position," Jocelyn rewound the voicemail to listen more carefully.

Her heart pounded as she realized what the message was: a job offer. Garrett, one of the best chefs in the culinary program, had graduated a year prior to Jocelyn but had made a huge impression on everyone. They'd all known he'd go far. And apparently he had: not only had he opened a very successful bistro in New York City, but he was opening up another location in San Francisco. And he wanted Jocelyn to be its new head chef.

It would be a huge opportunity. She'd get out of this small town, where she was limited on what she could make. Gwen had been as understanding and flexible as a boss could be, but Jocelyn couldn't cook the kinds of food that made her heart sing. She'd resigned herself to that fact when she'd moved here.

Yet she could be the head chef of a fine dining establishment in the heart of San Francisco.

But soon reality came crashing down. For one, she couldn't leave her dad. And, obviously, her husband. Luke wouldn't want to leave the island for his wife who wasn't really his wife.

Sighing, Jocelyn almost deleted the voicemail but at the last second archived it instead. She'd call Garrett tomorrow to let him know she was flattered but couldn't leave Hazel Island.

As she was about to leave Lyn's, another call lit up her phone.

"Bekah," said Jocelyn. "What's up? Why are you calling me so late?"

Bekah snorted. "Lola is finally in bed, that's why it's so late. And my heartburn is ridiculous right now. So I thought I'd call you to complain about it."

Jocelyn felt stupidly near tears. After Bekah had last texted her, angry at Jocelyn getting married without saying a word to her, the two friends had stayed mostly silent. Jocelyn had let Bekah's anger cool, hoping that her friend would forgive her.

Jocelyn swallowed against the lump in her throat. Bekah told her about her daughter Lola, how Elliot was doing, and how teaching was. As a marine biologist, Bekah would normally be out in the field doing research, but now that she was pregnant again, she was stuck on land.

"I can still sail," said Bekah. "I'm not that big yet."

"Remember that time you went out in a storm and nearly drowned?"

Bekah huffed. "Traitor."

"If you tried doing that, Elliot would tie you to a chair until you gave birth," joked Jocelyn.

"Don't give him any ideas. He's way too overprotective already."

Jocelyn waited for Bekah to ask her about Luke. When she finally did, Jocelyn could tell her friend was trying to sound as nonjudgmental as possible. Which, for Bekah, was never without a little bit of judgment. The woman simply couldn't help herself.

Jocelyn told Bekah that she and Luke had fallen into a routine, how life had settled into something mostly normal. She mentioned him trying to make her breakfast and how he'd bribed Fluffer into liking him.

Bekah was silent for a long moment. Then she said, "You sound happy."

"Do I?" Jocelyn tensed.

"Yeah, and it's making me worry about you. One second you hate the guy, and now you sound like totally infatuated." Her voice lowered as she added, "Have we forgotten how he treated you in high school?"

"Of course I haven't forgotten. But he explained why he acted like that. Aren't you the one who's always telling me to let things go?"

"I'm not saying holding grudges is healthy, but you can forgive without having amnesia."

"Look, I know you aren't happy that I got married without telling you, and I am sorry. You have no idea how sorry I am that I hurt you. But I need you to respect my decision, even if you don't understand it," said Jocelyn imploringly.

Bekah sighed. "I do support you. I'll always be your friend, but I reserve the right to be worried about you, too. I'm just afraid you're going to catch feelings for him."

"I'm not stupid enough to do that."

Bekah said nothing to that statement; she obviously didn't believe Jocelyn.

Trying to change the subject, Jocelyn mentioned the job offer from Garrett. "I won't accept it, though," she said.

"Why the hell not?"

Jocelyn was nonplussed. "Because I can't leave my dad? Or Luke?"

"Your dad I understand, although that could be worked around. But Luke? Girl, he's not even your legit husband. Why do you care about leaving him behind?"

Jocelyn's stomach twisted at Bekah's insinuation. "We have to show we're in love. If I leave without him, we won't get his inheritance."

"Long distance is a thing, you know. Elliot and I did it."

"For a few months. This thing could be for years."

"I'm just saying. Don't limit yourself because of this. And if Luke really cared about you at all, wouldn't he want you to be the happiest version of yourself?"

Jocelyn arrived back at the apartment with her mind whirling. She told herself she was declining the job offer solely for the inheritance, but a little voice of doubt niggled at the back of her mind.

Was it actually because the thought of being so far from her husband was too painful to contemplate?

CHAPTER EIGHTEEN

Luke and Jocelyn glanced at each other from across the dining table. Luke had only agreed to attend a dinner at the main house to keep his mom happy. He didn't know why his dad was even there: Gregory seemed like he'd rather be anywhere else than with his family.

Juliet's dogs sat at her feet, and she slipped them bits of meat as the meal progressed. Cosmo tried to go to Luke to beg, but Luke shooed the dog away. In revenge, it nipped at his ankle before returning to its mistress.

The dinner conversation was painful in its monotonousness. The same questions, the same answers. The same complaints about the weather, or the house, or the dogs. Juliet was perpetually complaining, while Gregory was perpetually irritated.

Luke wondered for the millionth time why his parents had stayed married when they so obviously disliked being in each other's company.

When Gregory began to talk about how his latest little

sports car needed a new part but he'd have to wait weeks to get it, Jocelyn shot Luke a wry look.

Weeks, mouthed Luke. *The inhumanity.*

Jocelyn lightly kicked him under the table, but she covered her mouth with her napkin to hide her laughter.

"It shouldn't take weeks for anything to ship," groused Gregory. "Anything longer than a few days is egregious."

"I'm assuming it has to be shipped from somewhere in Europe?" Luke asked idly.

"So?"

"Well, there are customs, and the distance—"

Gregory waved a hand. "No excuse."

Luke rolled his eyes. Jocelyn smiled at him.

That smile made his heart flip over in his chest. More and more, Luke had begun to count on his wife. Having her arrive home every evening from her job, having her in his bed, having her available to talk about small things and big things.

He realized in that moment, that unlike his parents, he liked being with his wife. And that, he knew, was an extremely dangerous development.

His thoughts were soon distracted when there was a brief commotion in the hallway outside the dining room. Gregory rose, muttering under his breath.

And then everyone went silent when none other than Tristan stepped into the room.

Luke couldn't move. For a split second, he hadn't recognized his brother, it'd been so long since he'd seen him. But then Tristan smiled, that sarcastic grin of his that he'd perfected as a teenager, a smile that Luke would recognize anywhere.

"Oh my God," said Juliet. She was the first one to approach Tristan. "Is it really you?"

"Hello, Mom. It's been a second."

Tristan allowed their mom to hug him, although Luke could tell he returned the gesture halfheartedly.

Luke also got up, but he didn't hug his brother. He shook his hand instead.

Tristan raised an eyebrow. "Bro." Then his gaze returned to the table. "Aren't you going to introduce me to your wife?"

Guilt instantly filled Luke. In the commotion, he'd forgotten about Jocelyn. She appeared at his side, though, and Luke introduced them in a hoarse voice.

Gregory hadn't gotten up. He stayed seated at the table, ignoring Tristan entirely.

Tristan, though, approached their dad to say, "Aren't you going to say hello?"

Gregory glanced at his son briefly. "You've made your entrance already. I don't need to add to it."

Tristan's jaw clenched. Luke waited for the inevitable blowup, but Tristan didn't take the bait. He sat down next to Juliet, who was still crying and barely able to speak.

"You really should've timed your entrance better," said Luke. "We've already finished eating."

Tristan ignored his brother. Instead, he turned his attention first to Juliet, then to Luke's annoyance to Jocelyn. Jocelyn looked especially pretty tonight: she wore a black dress, her hair in a French roll to show off her lovely shoulders.

Tristan was all charm as they finished eating. Jocelyn

even laughed at something he said, which made Luke want to stab his younger brother with a salad fork.

It didn't help that Tristan was no longer the gangly boy he'd been the last time Luke had seen him. He'd grown into a handsome man, confident and self-assured. And he seemed intent on flirting with Luke's wife right in front of him.

When Tristan touched Jocelyn's hand briefly, Luke stood to say dinner was over. "I want to speak with you," he said to Tristan. "Alone."

Before Luke went to his office to speak with Tristan, he said in Jocelyn's ear, "You'll be okay on your own?"

"I'll be fine. If all else fails, I'll hide in the bathroom. I doubt your parents will notice."

Luke kissed Jocelyn's cheek. She gave him an encouraging smile.

"This your office?" said Tristan after Luke had closed the door behind him. "When did you move into it?"

"A few years ago."

Tristan wandered around the room before going to stand by one of the windows. "What did you do with my art supplies?"

"I don't know. Mom took care of that."

"Probably threw them into the ocean."

Luke doubted that. More than likely Juliet had packed them away and they were gathering dust in the basement, where the rest of Tristan's things were. This room had been Tristan's art studio years ago, but after he'd run off, Luke eventually had chosen it for his office. It had the best natural light in the entire house.

Luke felt guilty for taking over the room, but he shoved the emotion aside.

"Why are you here?" said Luke. "And why did you have to be an asshole and make it a surprise? You could've called and made plans like a normal person."

Tristan grinned. "But what would be the fun in that? Besides, Dad would've told me to go to hell."

"Mom would've let you come." In a softer voice, Luke added, "She's missed you more than you know."

Tristan shrugged a single shoulder. He sat down in the one of the plush chairs, Luke occupying the other one. Tristan set his feet on a very expensive coffee table. It was as if he wanted Luke to know that he did not give a fuck about any of the wealthy trappings of his parents.

"I'm here for my money," said Tristan finally.

"Pretty sure you have to make up with the family, not just stop by for a sack of gold."

"And how is anyone going to quantify such a request? What, if Dad hugs me, then I get my money? It's bullshit."

"Granny wanted the family to heal."

"Forcing something like that never works. She just wanted to troll all of us." Tristan shot Luke a sly glance. "And you fell for it. You got married because dear ole granny said you were supposed to."

Luke stiffened. "Are you going to judge me for wanting my inheritance when you're doing the same exact thing?"

"At first I was, when I heard what you'd done. I couldn't believe it. I thought you had more spine than that, but I guess not. You've always been more inclined to dance to this family's tune than I was."

"One of us has to be responsible."

"Poor responsible Luke. What would happen if you weren't here?" Tristan laughed darkly. "Our parents might have to move to a smaller house. Oh no! Call the police. What a tragedy."

"I have other reasons. Not that I have to justify anything to you. I didn't run away when things got hard," snapped Luke.

Tristan's smile vanished. "Fuck off. You always had it easy. Don't try to tell me otherwise."

"Did you really come all the way here just to talk about the past? Because I'm not a therapist and I sure as hell am not going to listen to you whine for free."

"So you do have some spine. Touché, Bro."

"Tell me what you want already."

Tristan put up his hands. "I don't want anything from you. I told you why I'm here. And maybe I was curious about your wife. I vaguely remembered Jocelyn Gray from high school. I knew her sister, Alex. Weren't they poor kids?"

"So?"

"I'm just surprised the parents would let you marry a woman like Jocelyn, but I guess all of you were desperate. Then again, I can't blame you. She's a gorgeous woman. I'm sure fucking her isn't a chore."

Luke barely registered getting up, let alone taking his brother by his collar and shaking him. "You can insult me all you want," growled Luke, "but one word of disrespect for Jocelyn, and I'll break your fucking face."

Tristan's expression registered surprise. Then he laughed. "Oh, somebody's in their feelings. What a brave protector you are!" His voice was now an obnoxious singsong.

Luke let him go, albeit reluctantly. "Leave Jocelyn out of this."

"Fine, fine. Calm down. I'm not going to mess with her. But I have to say, I didn't expect you to get so pissed on her behalf." Tristan eyed him speculatively. "Do you love her?"

Luke scowled. Why did everyone insist on asking him that? "I respect her and want her to be treated well. That's all."

"Sure, sure. Whatever you need to tell yourself at night."

Luke didn't sit back down. He went to a window and gazed into the night. He wondered how Jocelyn was faring. And in that moment, he wanted nothing more than to take her into his arms and keep her safe. The thought of Tristan speaking poison into her ear, or something worse…

Luke turned. "Promise me you won't hurt Jocelyn. I've always been on your side, but not if you involve her. She's innocent. Whatever revenge you want on our parents, leave her out of it."

Tristan assessed him. "You really care about her."

"Was that a question?"

Tristan finally got up and held out his hand. "I have nothing against your wife, besides wondering what the hell is wrong with her, marrying into this family."

Luke took his brother's hand after a long moment. They shook, but Luke didn't feel much better. He hated that he couldn't trust his own brother.

Then, to his surprise, Tristan turned their handshake into a brief hug. "It's nice to see you," said Tristan roughly.

Luke froze, shocked, but returned the hug. Emotions he couldn't begin to unravel overwhelmed him.

"Likewise," said Luke quietly.

When Luke went to find Jocelyn, he felt like his world had been turned upside-down. With his brother back in the fold, Luke found himself looking at past events and emotions that he'd buried for years.

He wanted his wife. He wanted her comfort, her advice. Mostly, he wanted to sink into her body and lose himself.

"How did it go?" asked Jocelyn, concern on her face.

Luke pulled her into an embrace and hugged her hard. He knew in that moment he couldn't let her go.

"Let's go home," he said.

CHAPTER NINETEEN

Jocelyn hadn't been inside the Hazel Island bookstore in months. Alex had taken over the place a few years ago when the owner had wanted to retire. When Alex had told her about her buying the business, Jocelyn had been skeptical, telling Alex that it wouldn't be a great investment.

Alex, of course, hadn't taken the criticism well.

The bookstore, though, was extremely appealing when you stepped inside. There were colorful displays of books about Hazel Island immediately inside. Lots of sunlight filtered in through the large windows, while there were plush, comfy chairs to waste hours reading if you felt so inclined. The place had an open, friendly vibe.

Jocelyn remembered when Max had been the owner. He'd preferred to keep the place looking almost like a mausoleum, with curtains on the windows to keep out the light. The few chairs available had been uncomfortable. Despite it being uninviting, Max had done good business simply because during his tenure, it was the only place to buy books on the island.

Now with the popularity of eBooks and online ordering, the bookstore had suffered. Jocelyn didn't honestly know how her sister kept it going. Alex would never disclose the exact state of her business.

Another display in the store was a romance novel table. One big change Alex had enacted from the get-go was a wide selection of romance novels, something Max had turned his nose up to. Although Jocelyn had never been much of a romance reader, she had grown to respect why such a change had been important to Alex.

Jocelyn picked up the latest book by Lila White. Even Jocelyn, who didn't read romance, knew how popular this particular author was. And she always seemed to be releasing a new book. Jocelyn marveled that anyone could write that quickly.

"Have you read that one?" asked Alex.

"Will you throw me out if I admit I've never read one of her books?" admitted Jocelyn.

Alex clucked her tongue. "Jocelyn! Fail! I think you'd like them, even though I know you aren't a big romance fan." Alex plucked the newest release from Jocelyn's fingers. "But don't start with this one. Let me see if I can find *Protecting Her Heart.*"

After Alex had found a copy of the book she was looking for and had somehow persuaded Jocelyn to buy it, Jocelyn found herself tongue-tied. She'd barely spoken to her sister since that conversation in her car. They'd passed each other a few times in the street, but they'd acted more like acquaintances than siblings.

"How are you?" asked Jocelyn.

Alex had already started shelving some books, her back

turned to Jocelyn. "Fine. Busy. We're getting ready for an author signing this weekend."

When no more information was forthcoming, Jocelyn sighed internally. She said goodbye to her sister, feeling defeated, and headed out. But not before the mail carrier handed her the store's mail. The island was so small that everybody knew the mail carriers, and George knew that Jocelyn was the owner's sister.

Jocelyn hadn't intended to go through her sister's mail, but she couldn't help but notice red OVERDUE stamps on multiple envelopes. Just like on their dad's mail.

Jocelyn headed back to give her sister the mail, only for Alex to have disappeared again. Going to the back, Jocelyn went into Alex's tiny office, but her sister wasn't there.

On Alex's desk were more envelopes with the same OVERDUE notice on them. And on top was a letter stating that Alex would face eviction if she didn't pay her back rent immediately.

"What are you doing?" asked Alex from the doorway.

Jocelyn held up the letters. "What is this? Are you behind on rent?"

Alex immediately grabbed the letters, her cheeks turning red. "It's none of your business."

"Alex, is the bookstore in trouble?"

"I told you, it's not your business."

"It is when it affects our entire family. How can we help Dad when you can't pay your rent? This is serious!"

"You think I don't know that? I'm not stupid, despite what you always seem to imply."

The two sisters were both red-faced now. Jocelyn's frustration mounted in the face of her sister's opposition.

"I've never said you were stupid," Jocelyn ground out.

"Okay, maybe not stupid, but you've always made me feel like I couldn't be trusted to make any important decisions. You've always treated me like a child."

"Maybe because you keep acting like a fucking child!" Jocelyn's voice rose with each word.

Alex reared back. She was trembling now. "And you wonder why I didn't tell you? This is why! I don't need your judgment right now. I'll take care of it."

"How? By doing something idiotic like going to a loan shark? Because we both know you'd sign something without reading it—"

"Now you're just being an asshole—"

"And then guess what? I'll have to clean up the mess, just like I've always had to."

"I never asked you to clean anything up! You were the one who did that, and then you act like a martyr. No one asked you to be a martyr. That was something you took on of your own volition."

Jocelyn wanted to shake her sister. Her rage built: her frustration with her sister and their dad all twisted together until Jocelyn felt like she couldn't breathe.

"I've done everything to keep our family together," whispered Jocelyn, "and you did everything to destroy it."

Alex turned white now. "Because I bought a bookstore?"

"Because you make choices without considering the consequences. Do you know what happened when you disappeared that night? When you ran off with your boyfriend?"

"I was fifteen—"

"Dad was so upset that he had a stroke." Jocelyn was too

far gone to stop now. "He had a stroke because of *you*. It was your fault, Alex. Haven't you realized that?"

Alex was wide-eyed now. Tears brimmed in her eyes before falling down her cheeks.

"You seriously blame me for our dad having a stroke," murmured Alex, her voice choked. "Seriously?"

Far, far back in Jocelyn's mind, she knew she'd gone too far. She'd never allowed herself to be honest with her sister, but it was if the dam had lifted, and the rushing waters had consumed everything in its path.

"I said what I said," was Jocelyn's rough reply.

Alex lifted her chin. "I know you've never approved of anything I do. That's fine. But you think that if you can control everything around you, it'll make things safe. But you could never control me. And you hate me for it."

"I don't hate you."

"Bullshit. You blame me for everything that's gone wrong. Am I also the reason Mom left? Come on, lay it on me. We might as well get this all out in the open."

Jocelyn was dry-eyed. But she could feel tension running throughout her body and a headache beginning to form in her temples.

"Why are you bringing up Mom?" asked Jocelyn.

"Because she left, and you're still pissed! That's why. But she's not here, so you take it out on me."

"Seriously? You need to take responsibility of your own actions."

"I do! I do take responsibility. Just like when I bought this bookstore. I knew you didn't approve, but I did it anyway. I had a dream. I'm not going to apologize for trying." Alex wiped her eyes, but it didn't stop the flow of tears. "You ruined my life, too, you know. Did you never know that? I could've had that scholarship, but you were so angry that I defied you that you had your revenge."

Jocelyn stared, completely frozen. "You ran away. I had to ground you."

"And you had to tell my dance coach? You had to get me kicked off the team?" Alex shook her head. "No, you did that because you were angry, and it made you feel better. Well, congrats. You destroyed any chance I had of getting off this island. Ironic, considering we're now stuck here together."

Jocelyn felt like the earth beneath her feet was shifting. Most of all, she felt like her throat was closing. Shaking her head, she just kept saying, "I did it for your own good. I did it to protect you."

"Go home to your husband, Jocelyn. I'm tired of listening to you," said Alex quietly.

Jocelyn complied. She drove to the apartment, barely seeing where she was going.

She didn't cry. She felt like she should cry, but she didn't. Her heart was pounding hard, though, and after she walked through the door, she found herself slumping onto the couch.

She was shaking, she realized dazedly. Why should she be shaking?

"Jocelyn?" Luke was standing over her. "What's wrong?"

Seeing the concern in his eyes lifted whatever had been keeping her emotions in check. A moment later, she burst into tears, Luke's expression now one of complete shock.

CHAPTER TWENTY

Luke found himself at a loss. He froze, watching Jocelyn cry. No, not just cry—sob. Ugly, heart-wrenching sobs.

He didn't know what to do. When he tried to ask her what was wrong, she just shook her head and kept crying.

He sat down next to her and felt a little better when she let him put his arms around her. She buried her face in his shoulder as he made soothing sounds and rubbed her back.

After what felt like forever, the crying subsided. Jocelyn eventually lifted her face, which was red and tearstained, and tried to wipe her cheeks.

"Oh God, I got your shirt all wet," she moaned.

He'd barely noticed. "It's a shirt. It'll dry."

Jocelyn sniffled some more, which prompted Luke to bring her a roll of toilet paper. That gesture made Jocelyn smile.

"Do we not have any tissues?" she asked after she'd blown her nose.

"I could go get some."

That made her laugh. "No, it's not that serious. I just thought it was funny." She dabbed at her eyes. "Sorry about that."

Luke had never been comfortable around people crying. Especially women. He always had to restrain himself from running far, far away. Mostly because he'd learned early on that there was nothing you could do to stop the tears. You just had to wait it out.

"What happened?" asked Luke. When Jocelyn's eyes started to fill with tears again, he added quickly, "Not if you don't want to tell me—"

"No, no. I'll tell you." She took a deep, shuddering breath. "You know when talking makes you cry? Just give me a second."

Jocelyn soon composed herself as Luke waited. His chest hurt. Was this what it felt like, to really care about someone?

No, not just care. He cared about plenty of people. But the way he felt right now, seeing his wife in pain? It was agony. It made him want to find whoever had made Jocelyn cry and beat them to a pulp.

Jocelyn began to recount her argument with Alex. She had to pause multiple times to keep the tears at bay. With each word, Luke's anger with Alex increased.

By the time Jocelyn had finished, Luke was the one who had to compose himself before he said anything. He forced himself to unclench his fists and stop grinding his teeth. He'd certainly never hurt a woman, but at that moment, if Alex had walked through the door, he wasn't sure if he could control himself.

"She had no right to say those things to you," he said

roughly. "How could she be so selfish? When you've been the one taking care of the entire family?"

"Alex has always been the victim. Everything I did apparently was to make her life hell." Jocelyn looked mulish. "But did anyone ask me if I wanted to be her mother? No. I never wanted it, but our dad was working, and our mom was gone. So I had to."

Luke put his arm around Jocelyn's shoulders. "I get it. My younger brother is similar in a lot of ways to your sister. He still hates our parents for what they did to him. But he's an adult now. He should just get over it already."

"Younger siblings are a pain in the ass."

Luke chuckled. "I agree. Maybe there's something to be said about only having one kid, period."

After a long moment of silence, Jocelyn said quietly, "I was so angry with her. I didn't tell you everything. I said something that I've always kept inside." She wouldn't look at Luke now.

"I'm sure it wasn't that bad."

"I told her that I blamed her for our dad's stroke. Back when we were teenagers."

Luke stilled. He had a feeling there was more to this story than Jocelyn had let on. "I think I need context here."

Jocelyn soon launched into another story, one where a young Jocelyn had to act like a parent for a sister only five years her junior. Luke listened in growing dismay as she told him how Alex had gotten involved with an older boy, one who egged her on and spurred her to rebel further.

"I told her dance coach because I didn't know what else to do," Jocelyn said. "I didn't know how else to make Alex see sense. She was totally obsessed with this guy, but he was legally an adult. And she was fifteen. It was wrong. I don't care what anyone else says. It was wrong, and he was using her."

"That's a hard place to be in. Especially for someone that young," he said finally.

"I did what I thought was best, but maybe part of it was revenge. I don't know. I was so angry with Alex, because she was making our lives harder. *My* life harder. So maybe I was just being selfish." Jocelyn wiped her eyes. "Ugh, I can't keep crying. It'll just give me a headache."

"You were right to separate her from that guy. It sounds like he would've done worse to her."

"I don't regret that. But going to her coach… I don't know anymore. I've never regretted that until she said something. I guess she's been angry with me for years."

"Families are complicated."

That made Jocelyn snort. "Oh, you don't say? Mine is apparently extra complicated, though."

"Not any more complicated than mine." Luke mulled over his next words, wondering if he should even voice them. "Did you ever stop to think that maybe someone else is really to blame for all of this?"

"What are you talking about?"

Luke frowned. "Your dad. Where was he? He was the parent. Why did you have to be the one to deal with your sister?"

Jocelyn's expression turned cold. Luke had a feeling he'd overstepped, but he couldn't apologize for what he'd said, either.

"Our dad was busy working multiple jobs to keep us fed.

He did the best he could," said Jocelyn. She'd already moved away from Luke's embrace.

"Don't get defensive."

"You don't understand. You've never had to worry about money. My dad struggled, and as the oldest, I had to step up after our mom left. What else could we do?"

Luke could see Jocelyn getting agitated again. He made soothing noises, but she rebuffed them.

"You don't get to criticize my dad," she snapped. "He was a great dad. He took care of us. He loved us. He *stayed*. He could've left, too. Our mom had already abandoned us."

"Jocelyn, I'm sorry. Hush, please don't cry. I know you love your dad."

She let Luke take her into his arms, although she resisted at first. "But just because you love him," said Luke quietly, "doesn't mean he was perfect, either. Nobody is."

Jocelyn said nothing. She kept taking deep breaths, in and out, once again trying to compose herself. Guilt swamped Luke.

What had been the point of saying anything? Jocelyn wasn't ready to hear it. Maybe she never would be.

"Jocelyn, look at me." Jocelyn slowly raised her head. "I'm sorry. Forget what I said. I was talking out of my ass."

That made her lips quirk. "Seems like we're all doing that lately."

Luke couldn't help himself: he kissed her, tasting salt on her lips. She softened against him, and soon he was plunging his tongue into her mouth and touching every inch of her that he could reach.

"I don't think I can let you go," he admitted, his voice whisper-soft.

Jocelyn was still, and he wondered if he'd gone too far. But then she pulled him down for another kiss, and he felt his heart expand.

He carried to his bedroom. When he crossed the threshold, he couldn't help but think of her as his wife in truth. Based on Jocelyn's expression, she seemed to be thinking the same.

After they'd undressed each other, Luke drank in how beautiful she was. From her blond hair, to her long, swanlike neck, to her plump breasts and the little tummy below it. She had a few freckles scattered across her belly. He kneeled to kiss each one of them.

Jocelyn sighed and ran her fingers through his hair. "Luke," she sighed.

He parted her legs, needing to taste her with a desperation that was terrifying. He had her place one leg on the bed, giving him full access. When he began to lick, she shuddered and groaned.

She gradually grew wetter with each stroke of his tongue. When he fastened his lips around her clit, he could feel the tension coursing through her.

He knew he wouldn't last long once he was inside her. Pushing one finger inside her, he sucked her clit at the same time he massaged her sheath.

"Oh God!" Jocelyn was struggling to stay upright. "Oh my God!"

She came hard, screaming his name, and Luke drew out her release as long as he could. Then they were a bundle of limbs and sweaty skin on the bed. Jocelyn quickly rolled on top of him and sheathed herself on his cock.

"You're so fucking beautiful," he said, watching her bounce and roll on top of him. He played with her breasts as she rode him. She varied between quick bounces and simply rubbing her pelvis against his.

"Faster, baby," groaned Luke. His balls drew up, and he knew he was close to exploding. "Come for me one more time."

When he tweaked her nipples, she came with a loud shout. That was enough to send Luke over the edge. He pumped inside her sheath, releasing inside her until he was sure she'd squeezed every last ounce out of him.

Jocelyn collapsed on top of him. He held her close as she buried her face against his shoulder. When Luke hugged her so hard that her back popped, though, she sat up with a giggle.

"Are you my chiropractor now?" she asked.

"Lie back down and let's see if we can get some more pops."

She obliged, and Luke was able to get two more cracks that made Jocelyn laugh harder. Eventually she rolled off of him. Luke pressed his forehead to hers.

"I think I'm in love with you," said Luke, stroking her cheek.

Her eyes widened. When she said nothing in return, he nearly wished he hadn't said the words.

"I'm sorry," she stammered, "I should say them, too—"

"Not if you don't want to."

"No, no. I do." She swallowed. "I care about you. A lot."

Luke waited. Jocelyn squirmed before whispering, "I love you."

Her admission made him smile. Kissing her forehead, then her nose and finally her mouth, he said, "That wasn't so hard, was it?"

"Shut up."

He laughed, feeling happier than he'd ever remembered.

CHAPTER TWENTY-ONE

"Jossy, what are you doing in there? Are you making a five-course meal?" joked Pete from the living room.

Jocelyn wasn't making five courses, but she might've gone overboard in cooking for herself and her dad tonight. The meal included slow-roasted chicken, fingerling potatoes, and asparagus with a lemon-almond pesto. She'd even garnished their plates with roasted lemon slices that she knew her dad would never eat. Oh, and some brioche rolls; she'd made the dough the night before so it could proof overnight.

When she gave him his plate, his eyes widened appreciatively. "Quite a spread! Can't wait to taste everything."

If Jocelyn had made all of this food just to avoid having to talk about how her life was in shambles, she wasn't about to admit it. Then again, things with Luke had never been better.

After he'd found her sobbing, it was as if a final barrier between them had fallen. Jocelyn rejoiced, but she was also terrified. She'd told Luke she loved him.

It wasn't a lie—she *did* love him. But she hadn't been completely honest with him, either.

Jocelyn ate her food slowly, so slowly that her dad raised an eyebrow in question.

"Do you want any more? There's plenty," she said.

"No, and sit down. You have that look on your face that says you need to talk."

Jocelyn made a face. "I do not."

"You think I don't know my own daughter?" Pete pointed to the sofa. "Sit."

Jocelyn obeyed. Her dad rarely ordered them around. But when he did, she knew he meant business.

"Alex was here earlier, you know. She said you two fought," said Pete.

Jocelyn shrugged a shoulder. "That's hardly new."

"Maybe not, but she started crying just mentioning the topic. She refused to explain further. What the hell happened between you two now?"

Jocelyn's stomach twisted. She suddenly wished she hadn't eaten so much. "Did you know the bookstore's rent hasn't been paid in months?" she countered.

"No, but I'm not surprised."

"Neither am I. I told Alex that buying that place would be a money-sink. And look, I was right. We have your bills to pay, but she can't help. I'll have to be the one to dig everybody out of this—again."

With each word, her voice rose. She was so agitated that she wanted to tear her hair out. Instead, she picked out a thread on a throw pillow, yanking it out and finding another one to pull on.

"Your sister is an adult," said Pete quietly. "She bought

that store knowing it could go wrong. Did she ask you to give her money?"

Jocelyn scowled. "No, but you know how these things go with her."

"I think you're being overly harsh on her. And telling somebody 'I told you so' is never helpful, either."

Jocelyn yanked at the second thread, snapping it in two. "I'm tired of her never thinking about anyone but herself. Her choices affect all of us. She knows you need help, but she can't help. If she'd listened to me—"

Her dad held up a hand. "Jossy. I hear you. Your frustration is valid. But that's water under the bridge. Looking back and wishing something went differently won't change anything."

"I know that. I *know* that." Getting up, she went to sit on the ottoman in front of her dad. "I'm just…I'm tired. I'm so tired." Her voice broke.

"Sweetheart." Pete took her hands and squeezed them. His own voice was choked as he said, "You've always been the backbone of this family. I relied on you—too much. No, don't interrupt me. You were a child, too. I thought you were so mature, so responsible. But that doesn't make it right. I took your childhood from you by not stepping up as a parent."

"You did your best. You were keeping a roof over our head, food on the table—"

"I was, but I could've applied for other jobs. Something that allowed me to be home more." He sighed unhappily. "I got complacent. You were so reliable that I didn't even think about doing something different. That wasn't right. I'm sorry, sweetheart."

His apology made Jocelyn start crying again. She let herself be held, her heart breaking.

She didn't want to acknowledge that her dad—her hero, the man she'd looked up to her entire life—had failed her. It meant accepting that everyone could make mistakes. It meant that even if she tried to control every piece of her life, she would probably fail, too.

"I told Alex," said Jocelyn in a whisper, "that I blamed her for your first stroke."

Pete's forehead creased. "What…?"

"She was making our lives so stressful, and you were working all the time. I knew she was the straw that broke the camel's back."

Pete's voice was firmer now. "Your sister was a child. She didn't have a mom around and let's face it, a dad, either. And I had a stroke because I had the bad luck to get one. It probably didn't help that I smoked back in the day, either. Nobody's to blame for it."

Guilt made Jocelyn feel sick. She knew, in that moment, that she'd made a horrible mistake. "I think I've been taking out my anger on Alex all this time. When Mom left, Alex was my scapegoat."

Saying the words out loud felt bitter on Jocelyn's tongue, but also freeing. It meant that she could make amends and do better in the future. If Alex forgave her, though.

"Alex hasn't been an angel, either. She knows it, too." Pete's smile was wry. "Neither of my girls have been angels, but I didn't want angels. Angels are boring. You girls take risks, make mistakes, and get back up again. That's the Gray way."

Jocelyn smiled despite the sadness clouding her mind. "I

told Luke I was in love with him," she confessed out of the blue.

"Does he feel the same?"

"Yeah."

"You don't sound happy about it."

"I didn't lie to him, but he doesn't know about the bills. That I married him to help the family."

Pete frowned. "You need to be honest with him, then. Although it doesn't sound like you lied. You never said you loved him before now, right?"

Jocelyn shook her head. "No, I could never do that."

Despite her dad's assurances, though, Jocelyn wasn't sure. If Luke didn't believe her, if he decided that he really didn't love her after all, she'd be devastated.

"You have to be brave, Jossy," said Pete before she left for the evening. "And I know you can be. You're the bravest person I know."

Luke hesitated, his fist hanging in the air. He hadn't thought this plan through entirely. When he'd driven over here, he'd only wanted to see if he could get some answers.

Mostly, he wanted to talk with his father-in-law. Luke knew he'd been a jerk for not seeing him before now.

Before Luke knocked, though, he heard a woman's voice say behind him, "Hello?"

He turned to see Alex coming up the walkway. She cocked her head to the side, a gesture that was so similar to Jocelyn that Luke had to restrain a smile.

The two sisters didn't look alike, though. Where Jocelyn

was fair, Alex was dark. Where Jocelyn was slender, Alex was curvy. They both had similarly shaped eyes and the same stubborn chin, Luke noticed.

"What are you doing here? Are you looking for Jocelyn?" asked Alex.

"I wanted to talk to your dad."

Alex was instantly suspicious. "Why? Where's Jocelyn?"

"She doesn't know I'm here."

Alex crossed her arms over her chest. "What shady shit are you trying to pull?"

That remark made Luke chuckle. "Can't a son-in-law stop by to see his father-in-law?"

"Have you even met my dad?"

Luke grimaced. "In passing. It's a small island."

Alex's eyes were still narrowed, but she didn't tell him to get lost. It was a nice day, the breeze blowing in from the ocean to keep the day from getting too warm. Alex gestured for Luke to follow her.

Not into the house, but to the backyard, where a rickety table and chairs sat. They'd clearly seen better days: the metal was rusty, the cushions sun-bleached. Luke wasn't sure what color they had once been.

"Why are you here?" said Alex without preamble.

"You're very direct, you know."

"My sister is worse. So you should be used to it by now. Answer the question."

"I told you. I wanted to see your dad."

"He's busy. He also doesn't like visitors."

"I'm not a visitor. I'm family."

At that, Alex shot him an annoyed look. "Since when? You and my sister get married without telling anybody, you haven't seen my dad since then, and now you just stop by like it's no big deal?"

"Shouldn't I have this conversation with him?"

Alex raised her chin. "I don't like you, Luke Wright. I don't trust you as far as I can throw you."

That made Luke raise an eyebrow. "I think you're the more direct sister. Also, you don't know me."

"I know *about* you. I know that you hurt my sister years ago and that she despised you up until recently. When my sister hates somebody, she really hates somebody. Yet you somehow managed not only to get her to agree to marry you, but to convince her you were a nice guy. But I see right through you."

"Those bodies you found in our backyard aren't mine," replied Luke wryly.

Alex ignored his attempt at a joke. "I'm not letting you see our dad because you'll pull the wool over his eyes. He's way too inclined to like people."

"And you aren't?"

"Most people aren't worth liking."

"You're too young to be so cynical."

Alex's mouth twisted. "Age has nothing to do with it."

"And here I thought you were just a cute little bookstore owner. My sister-in-law has claws, apparently."

"I'm not your sister-in-law."

"I'm married to your sister. So, yes, you are." Luke gave her a confused look. "Unless I missed some memo?"

"You aren't my brother-in-law because we both know this marriage isn't going to last. Jocelyn will come to her senses, just like she did back in high school."

Now Luke was starting to get irritated. "Look, I didn't

come here to be interrogated. If you want to think badly of me, that's on you."

"I want to know what you're planning to do in regard to my sister." Alex's voice rose. "She comes off as so strong and capable, but she isn't. Not always. But she'll grin and bear things until she falls apart. I'm not going to let you hurt her."

Luke blinked in astonishment. To his further surprise, Alex was now blinking away tears.

His ire faded away right then. "You're afraid for her," he said softly.

"I'm not afraid."

"Have you said these things to her?"

Alex laughed sadly. "No way. She'd never believe me. We got into a really bad fight recently. Did she tell you about it?"

"She might've mentioned it," hedged Luke.

"She told me off. I deserved it." Alex swiped at her tears. "But I'm also still pissed at her. Oh, it's complicated. You know, so often I want to run my sister over, but if I hear anyone wanting to hurt her, I want to run *them* over. It's weird. I'm sorry, I'm not making any sense."

"You make a lot of sense. Too much, honestly."

The two sat in silence, watching a flock of crows fly in circles above a tall pine tree. One crow landed in the yard, picked up something shiny, and promptly flew back to the tree.

"You know, I started feeding the crows that come around the bookstore," said Alex. "Now they know me and follow me around the island."

"That's impressive."

She smiled, shrugging. "Nothing some bribery can't accomplish."

Luke picked his next words carefully. He knew as well as anyone that getting in the middle of family feuds could end badly.

"Jocelyn was really broken up after your fight," he said, watching another crow fly into the yard and hop around.

"She didn't seem broken up when she left."

"She doesn't like to be vulnerable in front of people."

Alex's gaze met his. "But she was in front of you." Then she looked away. "Huh."

To Luke's amusement, Alex reached inside her pocket and took out a bag of peanuts, still shelled. When she saw his look, she chuckled. "Yeah, I always carry peanuts now."

She began tossing the peanuts into the yard. The single crow at first didn't see the peanut, but a second swooped down to snag it. The first crow cawed, as if annoyed. Alex tossed it a peanut. Soon, there were over a dozen crows in the yard. Most of them did their best to collect as many peanuts as possible they could in their beaks. Three peanut shells were apparently the maximum these crows could carry at a time.

"Look, I get sibling issues," said Luke. "My brother and I barely have a relationship, so I'm not going to judge you and Jocelyn. But I'll just say that I wish I could count on my brother like you can count on your sister."

Alex was quiet. Soon she was out of peanuts, and the crows eventually dispersed. One, however, stayed sitting on the fence to watch them. Luke could almost believe the bird could understand what they were saying.

"Jocelyn has taken care of me since I was little. All of

us, really. And now with our dad's bills piling up, she's had to carry another burden."

At the mention of bills, the hair on the back of Luke's neck stood on end. He couldn't help but think of Tristan's remark a few days ago. *I have nothing against your wife, besides wondering what the hell is wrong with her, marrying into this family.*

But Jocelyn loved him. She'd told him so. He had no reason not to believe her.

"Is your dad in debt?" asked Luke.

"Well, let's just say there was a possibility of him losing the house."

"And now there isn't?"

Alex stilled, but then she just said, "I'm sure my dad is looking for me."

"Tell him I said hello."

Luke sat in the backyard for a few more minutes. The crow sitting on the fence was still watching him. It was so still that if Luke hadn't seen it flying earlier, he might've thought it was a mannequin.

He'd always known that Jocelyn hadn't loved him when they'd married. He'd assumed it was for his money. But now that he loved her and she'd said the same, he couldn't help but wonder if she was lying.

She might've said the words solely to keep the marriage intact. She needed the money, after all—desperately, if Alex was to be believed.

When he finally got up, the crow flew away, its dark plumage streaking across the sky like an omen.

CHAPTER TWENTY-TWO

When Kelly told Jocelyn there was someone at the restaurant who wanted to see her, she assumed it was Luke. But when Jocelyn headed toward the small area near the supply closets and bathrooms, she found her brother-in-law instead.

After Jocelyn had been assured Luke was okay, she told Tristan that she was too busy to talk.

"This can't wait," he said.

Jocelyn glanced over her shoulder. It was only an hour until the restaurant would close to prepare for the dinner service. Reluctantly, Jocelyn let Kelly know she'd be in her office and ushered Tristan in that direction.

"I've only been back a few days," said Tristan, "but I've already heard great things about this place."

"Then you should come by to try it sometime."

Tristan shook his head. "I won't be in town long."

"That's a shame. I know Luke was happy you'd returned. I'm sure your parents were, too."

At the mention of his parents, Tristan's expression closed. Although Luke had disclosed some of the reasons why his younger brother was angry with his parents, much of it remained a mystery to her. She wished Alex were here. She could get the information out of Tristan.

"So, did you just come by to tell me you've heard good reviews of my restaurant?" said Jocelyn.

"I wanted to see you without Luke around."

At that admission, Jocelyn suddenly wished she hadn't closed the door. Tristan, though, didn't move from his chair. He seemed lost in thought. Jocelyn didn't have any inkling that he was a threat to her safety.

You're just being paranoid, she told herself. *He doesn't even know you.*

"When I heard Luke had gotten married, I wasn't surprised, you see. But when I found out it had to do with getting his inheritance, well, I had to come meet the woman in person. It'd take a special kind of person, you know, to marry a guy just in the hope that he got a fat check by the end of it," said Tristan.

Jocelyn had to fight to retain her composure. Despite that, her cheeks reddened. "What are you implying?"

"Nothing. I'm *saying* that you married my brother for his money."

"So you came down here just to insult me."

Tristan smiled, but there was no mirth in it. "I don't mean any insult. I think it's impressive. Coldblooded, but money does that to people. I include myself in that circle. I've only come back to get what's owed me."

"Again, I don't understand why you felt the need to come down here to tell me this."

"You're very direct, aren't you? I like that. I was afraid Luke's wife was going to be some society girl who'd do whatever it took to suck up to the family. But not you. You don't really give a shit what my parents or what I think, do you?"

Jocelyn just waited, a single eyebrow raised.

"I don't blame you for wanting Luke's money. If you two had made a deal with each other, that's on you." Tristan stood up now. He was tall—taller even than Luke. Jocelyn hated that she had to tilt her head back to keep eye contact. "But I also know that my brother loves to play the savior. He's not good at it, but he's always been that way. And I saw how he acted when I mentioned your name."

Jocelyn felt her blood freeze in her veins. "How?"

"He cares about you. He might even be in love with you." Tristan assessed her. "That's not a surprise to you, then."

"You sound upset that your brother has feelings for his wife."

"I'm upset that a woman who married my brother is now manipulating him to think that she cares about him. When you're going to dump him as soon as that check is signed. You're going to screw him for everything he's worth. And my brother might be an idiot, but I'm not going to stand by and see him get fucked, either."

Jocelyn moved so she was now standing near the door. "I think you've said more than enough. I have to get back to work."

"If you really cared about Luke, you'd let him go. But we all know you're not going to do that. We're not so different, you and me. We both had to become coldhearted assholes to survive."

Jocelyn's smile was tremulous. "We're nothing alike. Now, please leave."

Tristan stared at her, as if surprised she wasn't sobbing incoherently. Then he shrugged and walked out of her office without another look.

JOCELYN RETURNED to the apartment late that night—so late that she expected Luke to be asleep already. To her surprise, he was sitting on the couch. He wasn't watching TV, though. Fluffer sat on his lap, and he was stroking him absently.

"Did you wait up for me?" said Jocelyn. "You didn't have to."

"I couldn't sleep."

There was something in his voice that set her on edge. It reminded her all too well of what Tristan had said. Had that only been this afternoon? It felt like a thousand years ago.

Jocelyn sat down, although she desperately wanted to take a shower and get into her pajamas. Luke had his glasses on, but he hadn't changed out of his jeans yet. She wondered if he'd even tried to go to bed.

Before Jocelyn could recount her conversation with Tristan, Luke said, "Tell me about your dad's bills."

The question was innocuous enough, but Jocelyn heard that same strange note in Luke's voice.

"He has a lot of them. That tends to happen when you get sick," she hedged.

Luke still wasn't looking at her. Fluffer's eyes were closed, but they snapped open when Jocelyn reached out to pet him. The rabbit hopped away to the opposite side of the couch, taking the stairs down to go sit in his bed near the TV.

"Rejected," said Luke. Then he looked at Jocelyn. "I talked to your sister today."

"Alex? Why?"

"I wanted to see your dad, but she wouldn't let me into the house. She's terrifying, by the way."

That comment made Jocelyn chuckle. "She can be."

"She loves you. She defended you, even. I was surprised. You made it sound like she hated you."

"She defended me?" Jocelyn was incredulous. "That's hard to believe."

"She told me point-blank that she didn't like me." He chuckled. "Told me I was shady. Which is hilarious, because what did I find out but that my wife was keeping some secrets from me? Big secrets."

Jocelyn swallowed. She hated that Luke felt so distant. Where had that man who'd told her he loved her gone? She didn't recognize this person.

"You know as well as I did that we didn't get married in the beginning for love," she said.

"Oh God." Luke dropped his head into his hands. "I knew it. I told myself, over and over again, not to let myself fall for you because you hated me. You don't love me, do you? You only married me for the money."

His voice was like a whiplash. Jocelyn flinched, but she also felt her own anger rising.

"Okay, I married you for the money. I was desperate. Not only was my dad drowning in medical debt, but he's also close to losing his house. There's no money to send him to a decent nursing home. He would've ended up in some terrible place far from here. I couldn't let that happen—"

Luke raised a hand. "It doesn't matter. I should never have been stupid enough to believe you'd want me for myself."

"I didn't—I mean, I don't know—"

"How am I supposed to believe that? Saying that you care about me is the best way for us to stay married and for me to get my inheritance."

"Luke! Listen to yourself." Jocelyn scrambled up from the couch, so quickly that it startled Fluffer. She soothed the rabbit and then took him to his cage for the night.

When she returned, Luke was gone. She saw that his bedroom door was shut. Going to it, she tried the knob, but it was locked.

"Luke! Don't do this. Please!"

"Go to bed, Jocelyn. It's late. I'm tired."

She pressed her forehead to the door. She started to shake. Most of all, she could hear Tristan's words inside her head.

If you really cared about Luke, you'd let him go.

She nearly fell to the floor when Luke wrenched the door open. He caught her just in time but let her go a moment later.

"Are you saying we're over?" she whispered.

Luke was dry-eyed, his expression without emotion. "I

don't know. But I also know I can't keep living a lie. Not even for the money."

He gently shut the door in her face. In a fit of rage, she swore and kicked at it. Luke, though, didn't open it a second time.

Jocelyn climbed into her cold bed, the tears finally coming in torrents, and she cried until she fell into a fitful sleep.

CHAPTER TWENTY-THREE

Dinner service that night was not going well. Mistakes kept being made, and when a burger was sent out with onions a second time, Jocelyn lost her temper.

"Can we have some quality control around here?" she burst out. She zeroed in on Kelly, who had been the one tasked to double-check the burger. "Come with me."

Kelly made a face but eventually followed Jocelyn. With her arms crossed and her expression smug, Kelly just made Jocelyn's anger worsen.

"What will it take to get you to care about your job?" said Jocelyn.

"What do you mean? I'm here, aren't I?"

"Just being physically present doesn't count. Don't you care about the food you're serving to customers? Because it seems like you don't give a shit about this job or becoming an actual chef."

"You're always harping on me. It's not my fault you can't control your own kitchen. You're the boss." Kelly's tone was snide.

"You know what?" Jocelyn smiled without humor. "You're fired. Get your things and leave."

Kelly gaped at her. "Seriously?"

"Completely. I'd rather have no sous chef than have one like you. Now get out."

Kelly's eyes filled with tears, but Jocelyn was unmoved. She didn't have time to coddle anyone right now.

When Jocelyn returned to the kitchen, she announced that Kelly was no longer employed at the restaurant and that was that. Although the staff darted glances at each other, none were brave enough to comment.

The dinner service was arduous without a sous chef, but Jocelyn reveled in it. She'd needed the distraction of work. She wished she'd fired Kelly months ago.

Luke would've fired her way earlier, her mind whispered.

Jocelyn pushed the thought aside. Thinking about Luke just sent her emotions into a tailspin. It didn't help that she dreamed about him nearly every night.

Sometimes the dreams were happy, with him coming to her dad's house and telling her he was wrong. Other dreams were nightmares, where he told her he'd never loved her and never would. He'd only wanted her to get his inheritance. How could she have been so stupid to think otherwise?

As dinner service began winding down, Gwen came back. She pulled Jocelyn into the walk-in fridge for some privacy.

"I heard you fired Kelly," she said in a low voice.

"I did." Jocelyn raised her chin. "I know you wouldn't approve."

"Since when? You've never liked her. Were you really letting her stay to please me?"

Jocelyn was nonplussed. "Yes. No. I don't know." Sighing, she rubbed the back of her neck. "I think I was afraid of being seen as a coldhearted bitch who just can't get along with anybody."

"You're not a coldhearted bitch. You can be intimidating, but that's not a bad thing. I've always envied that about you."

"Really?"

"Yeah. You take the bull by the horns. You don't let people walk all over you. And if you were a man, nobody would criticize you for it."

Jocelyn's lips twisted. "True."

Gwen cocked her head to the side. "How are you? Really?"

Jocelyn felt that ever-present lump in her throat form. "I'm fine. Really. I'll survive just like I always have."

"Surviving isn't living."

"What else can I do? Luke wants to think the worst of me, and that's his prerogative. I'm not going to beg him to take me back."

"Of course not. No one wants you to. He's the one who needs to come groveling."

"Since that will never happen, I'm moving on with my life." Jocelyn swallowed hard. "I've already filed for divorce."

Gwen's eyes widened. "Seriously?"

"Luke should be served by Monday next week."

Gwen just stared at Jocelyn, making her uncomfortable.

"What?" snapped Jocelyn. "Say what you want to say."

"I just… I didn't think you'd get divorced. It's only been a month. Maybe Luke will want to reconcile—"

"I'm not waiting around for him to get his head out of his ass."

Gwen's shoulders slumped. "No, of course not. That wouldn't make sense. I'm just sad for you. I'm even sad for Luke."

"You're a nicer person than I am."

Gwen's smile was sad. She squeezed Jocelyn's shoulder. "I should let you get back to work. I'm not paying you to have therapy sessions in the walk-in fridge, after all."

ON THE DAY Luke would be served the divorce papers, Jocelyn came over to Alex's for dinner. It'd been Alex's idea for Jocelyn to come over.

Jocelyn hadn't been in Alex's tiny studio apartment very often. More often than not, they'd seen each other at their dad's. Despite its size, the apartment was filled with colorful posters, weird statues, and plants. So many plants. Jocelyn marveled that her sister could fit so much greenery in there.

Alex didn't have a kitchen table, so the two sisters sat on her couch in the living room. Jocelyn sipped her wine and waited.

The two sisters hadn't talked much since their fight a month ago. Jocelyn hadn't had the emotional energy since her marriage with Luke had ended. She felt guilty about it, though. She should've been the one to invite her sister out for lunch or coffee.

"I have news," said Jocelyn.

"I hope it's good news."

"For once, it is." Jocelyn took a deep breath. "I accepted a job offer. In San Francisco. I'll be starting in a month, moving there in two weeks."

Alex gaped. "What? You're leaving Hazel Island? Have you told Gwen yet?"

"Not yet. I just accepted the offer today. I'll put in my notice later this week."

"I can't believe you'd leave Lyn's. You and Gwen started it together."

Jocelyn swirled her wine. "You don't need to make me feel even guiltier. But I need to get out of here. I'm sure I don't need to explain why."

The sisters fell silent. Soft music flowed around them, along with the ticking of a cuckoo clock on the wall. Except instead of a bird, a skeleton would pop out when the clock struck the top of the hour.

"The thing is, I don't want to leave if you don't want me to," said Jocelyn. "Because of Dad. I don't want to put that burden on you."

"He has his nurse. Although what about money…"

"My new job will be paying me nearly double what I'm getting at Lyn's. The cost of living is higher, of course, but I can find a cheap place in the area. Get some roommates. Maybe rent a cardboard box if I'm lucky," Jocelyn joked.

"So that's it, then. You'll be leaving us. What about Luke?"

Jocelyn's fingers tightened around the stem of her wineglass. "He should've received divorce papers today."

"Oh."

Jocelyn didn't want to talk about Luke. She would've preferred to talk about anything other than the fact that her husband had broken her heart. Or how he hadn't spoken to her in a month besides a few polite texts here and there. They weren't even friends anymore; that hurt almost as badly.

"Before I move, though, I wanted to tell you that I'm sorry for what I said that day. It wasn't fair. You weren't to blame for Dad's stroke. You were only a kid," said Jocelyn.

Alex's lower lip quivered. "Thank you."

"I know I've been hard on you. Probably too hard. You aren't stupid or a failure. You take risks. You're not afraid of everything like I am."

"You? Afraid? Bullshit."

"Terrified. I think I've been reacting in fear since Mom walked out on us. If I could control everything around me, we'd be okay. But life doesn't work like that, and people definitely don't."

"I always felt like you hated me," whispered Alex.

"No, of course not."

"Like if you could've gotten rid of me, your life would've been better."

Jocelyn's heart twisted. Setting their wineglasses down, she pulled her sister into a hug.

"You frustrated the hell out of me, but I was terrified of you getting hurt. But I was a kid, too. I didn't know what I was doing most of the time," said Jocelyn.

Alex sniffled. "I'm going to figure out a way to save the bookstore. I don't want you to be the only way to help take care of Dad."

"It's fine."

"No, it's not. You were right: you have been cleaning up my messes. But not anymore. Even if I burn the place down, it's my problem. You don't need to worry about me, okay?"

Jocelyn couldn't promise that, exactly, but she nodded anyway.

"Do you love him?" asked Alex quietly.

Jocelyn stared at nothing. "Does it matter?"

"You know, when I met with him, he talked about you didn't like to seem vulnerable. But that you were with him. I realized that he might know my sister better than I did. It hurt, but I was happy for you, too. You deserve a guy who adores you."

"So do you."

"I'm sorry Luke turned out to be a loser. I really thought things would end differently."

Jocelyn's smile was sad. "Me too."

"About my dance scholarship…" When Jocelyn opened her mouth, Alex held up a hand. "I get why you did it. I don't agree with it, but you were trying to keep me safe."

Alex's eyes clouded. "I thought I was in love with Jason, you know. He was so cute, and he gave me all these little gifts. He'd write me notes, telling me how pretty I was."

"He gave you the attention you weren't getting at home," said Jocelyn.

"Probably. I dreamed about us getting married. So when you made us break up, I was so angry. I hated you so much."

"I know."

"I just wanted to say that you did the right thing."

Alex opened her mouth to say something else when the cuckoo-skeleton clock sounded. Both sisters jumped, then laughed at themselves.

"I'm hungry," said Alex suddenly. "Let's order something before I turn into a hangry monster."

CHAPTER TWENTY-FOUR

Luke stared at the documents that had just been delivered. He'd been tempted not to sign for them, but he knew it would've been pointless.

Jocelyn had filed for divorce. Her signature was scrawled at the bottom of the page. It seemed accusing. Or maybe it just wanted to remind him of what he lost.

Luke threw the papers onto his desk. If he could burn them, he would.

He began to pace his office. He'd returned to the Wright mansion soon after Jocelyn had moved out of their apartment. Luke didn't know which had been more of a torment: being around his family or knowing that Jocelyn would never return to the place they'd called home.

The only benefit of the mansion was that it was so large Luke could avoid his family. And avoid he did. He didn't go down for dinners. When he did happen to run into one of them, he kept conversation to a minimum.

His dad had already done his best to guilt-trip him for failing in his marriage.

"You've already thrown in the towel?" Gregory had shouted when Luke had moved back. "It's been two months!"

"She's gone. Do you want me to drag her back?"

"If that's what it takes!" Gregory had grabbed Luke by the arm. "That money is ours. You have a duty to me and your mother. To this family. Stop acting like a child and do whatever it takes to get your wife back."

Luke had thrown off his dad's hold and had stalked away.

Luke had too much pride to go after Jocelyn. Besides, she wasn't who he thought she'd been. What was the point of continuing the charade when everyone knew it was over?

Luke had expected Opal to contact him, but he hadn't heard a peep from her. To his immense amusement, he'd discovered that she'd traveled to Italy soon after Jocelyn had left, and she wasn't expected to return for another month.

Luke would've thanked his lucky stars for the respite, except it only delayed the inevitable. Opal would find out the jig was up. He wondered, for the first time, what would happen to his inheritance now.

Granny must've made a provision in her will. He'd just been so preoccupied with getting his hands on it he hadn't thought about what would happen if he'd failed. He hoped Granny had chosen well.

Luke had tried to get some work done, but the divorce papers being served had interrupted him. Now, all he wanted to do was drink his sorrows away.

Luke swirled the liquor in his glass, wondering what the hell he was going to do now. He'd already pledged a decent percentage of the inheritance to a few organizations. He wasn't looking forward to informing them that he didn't actually have the money.

There wouldn't be any funding to help clean up the beaches around Hazel Island or to protect endangered wildlife like orcas and salmon. There wouldn't be funding to produce more green energy.

He sighed. He'd just have to find another way to get the money. It wasn't that Luke was averse to hard work. It was just that his inheritance was so large it could've helped a lot of people, including his own parents.

"Is this how you're spending your time now? Staring out windows and brooding?"

Luke heard Tristan approach but didn't turn to greet him. His younger brother hadn't been particularly sympathetic when he'd learned about Jocelyn leaving Luke.

"You're the one who's perfected brooding," said Luke.

Tristan went to the bar and poured himself his own drink and went to join Luke. The sunset streaked across the sky, and there was a full moon already on the horizon.

Luke couldn't help but think that Jocelyn would've loved this sunset. He wondered if she were looking up at the sky right now.

"So, I'm leaving," said Tristan finally.

"You don't have to ask me permission to go hang with your friends, you know."

"I mean, I'm heading out. For good."

Now Luke did look at his brother. "'For good'? So you're going to disappear for years without a word? At least add me on Facebook, would you?"

Tristan scowled and downed his glass of what looked

like a gin and tonic. "I don't know. I just know I can't stay another day in this house. It's fucking haunted."

Luke laughed. "Haunted? Have you seen a ghost in your room?"

"Not literally. But the energy in this house…" Tristan rolled his eyes. "Stop laughing at me. You know what I mean."

Luke sobered. "I do. Even better than you would, considering how much longer I've spent living here."

Tristan said nothing to that. He watched a bird circle and then begin flying west. "I don't know how I'm supposed to get my money. I've decided it's not worth the effort."

"Oh, really? You're giving up already?"

"You're one to talk. Your marriage lasted, what, two months?"

Luke wished it were socially acceptable to toss younger brothers out of windows. Instead, he said, "Have a nice trip. Where are you going, by the way?"

"I don't know yet."

"Well, send me a postcard when you get to wherever it is."

Luke went to his desk, ignoring Tristan, not feeling interested in engaging him further. He didn't need another family member reminding him that he'd failed everyone.

"Luke, I need to tell you something."

Luke was barely listening. "What?"

"It's about Jocelyn."

At hearing her name, Luke stilled. Just hearing her name sent an arrow straight through his heart.

"What about her?"

"I saw her, the day you two broke up. I went to talk to her myself."

Luke felt like all the oxygen in the room had disappeared.

"And why would you do that?" Luke's voice was deadly soft.

"I haven't been a great brother. I know that. But neither of us should have to upend our lives just for some money. Granny making you get married is bullshit. You should never have done it. You should've told our parents fuck off."

"What did you say to Jocelyn?" Luke felt suddenly sick to his stomach. "Did you do something to her?"

Tristan at least looked outraged at that suggestion. "Fuck you, man. I didn't touch her. I'm not a monster."

"Tell me before I rip your goddamn guts out."

"I'm trying to. Jesus Christ." Tristan ran his fingers through his hair. "I told her that I was onto her, that's all. That she only wanted your money and that she should let you go."

"You told her that."

"Yeah, that's it. I swear."

"Why are you telling me this now?"

"Because maybe it'd mean something. Or because I've seen how fucking miserable you've been since she left you and I wondered if I'd made a mistake."

That made Luke laugh. "You admitting you made a mistake? Wonders never cease."

"Yeah, I fucked up. Is that what you wanted to hear? But I did it because I was looking out for you."

Luke just shook his head. Picking up the divorce papers, he handed them to Tristan.

"Well, thanks for your confession, but it's still over. I got these today."

"Shit."

"So I guess Jocelyn listened to you. She let me go."

Tristan said nothing. He was staring at the papers like they contained the secrets of life itself.

"This is a sign," said Tristan.

"A sign?"

"Fuck. Fuck, fuck, fuck!" Tristan looked wild-eyed now. "I didn't know that she loved you. I swear. I thought she was just using you."

Luke sighed. "It doesn't matter."

"Yeah, it does!" Tristan pushed the papers into Luke's hands. "She's not getting a penny now. She could've kept sweet and lied her ass off to keep the marriage going. She didn't. Who would do that if not somebody who gives a shit?"

"I ended things. She had no choice."

"Bullshit. If she'd shown up here, telling you she loved you and wanted to make things work, you're telling me you would've sent her packing?"

Luke shook his head. "I don't know."

"At least go talk to her." Tristan's expression turned haunted. "I know what it's like to lose the woman you love forever. You don't have to be like me. *Go get her already.*"

Excitement was like a drumbeat inside Luke's chest. He suddenly ripped the divorce papers in half, and it was like ropes tying him down were loosened.

"I love her," said Luke simply. "I'm going to get her back."

Before he left, he gave Tristan a brief, tight hug. Tristan sighed, but he returned the hug a moment later.

CHAPTER TWENTY-FIVE

Luke arrived at the restaurant to find that Jocelyn wasn't there. Jack stopped him from going back into the kitchen with a black look.

"What the hell are you doing here?" his friend demanded.

"Not that it's any of your business, but I need to talk to my wife."

Jack's expression turned to one of confusion. "She's leaving. Didn't you know?"

"Leaving? What, she's going on a trip?"

"No… She's moving. She got a job in the Bay Area."

Luke felt like his entire world was crashing down around him. "She's leaving Hazel Island? The restaurant? Her dad? There's no way. You must've heard wrong."

"Well, she put in her notice with Gwen, so my source is pretty reliable."

Luke realized that he was starting to make a scene. A number of people sitting at tables were staring at him and Jack.

Luke took Jack outside. "Do you know where she is? Or is she already gone?"

"Don't you have her phone number?" groused Jack.

"She's not answering my texts or calls!"

Jack gave him a strange look, and Luke wanted to rip out his hair when his friend said nothing for a long moment.

Then: "You love her."

"For fuck's sake, of course I love her!"

"Well, you've done a shit job of showing her. She's been a mess since you guys broke up. Gwen kept saying that it was like Jocelyn had disappeared and some robot had taken her place."

Luke felt guilt, but also hope, at that statement. It meant that Jocelyn still cared. Maybe, in time, she could grow to love him again. She could forgive him for being a complete asshole.

"I fucked up," admitted Luke. "It doesn't matter how. I just have to tell her before she goes."

Right then, Gwen came outside. "Oh, Luke. Hello."

"Gwen, do you know where Jocelyn is?"

"She's probably at home packing. She's catching the two o'clock ferry today. Or was it the one o'clock? I can't remember."

Luke glanced at his watch. It was a half hour to one. The ferry was only a ten-minute car ride from the center of town.

"I have to go." Before he ran off, though, he said to Jack and Gwen, "If you see her, tell her I love her."

Gwen sighed happily. "Then you better go find her! Go, go!"

Luke didn't need to be told twice. His mind was racing as he got back into his car and drove to Jocelyn and Pete's place.

She'd taken a job in San Francisco? He hadn't even known she'd been looking. Why hadn't she told him? *Probably because she didn't feel like you'd understand.*

He hated that his wife felt like she couldn't tell him things. If she wanted to pack and move to California, fine. He'd follow her. He'd follow her to the ends of the earth if necessary.

When he arrived at the house, he saw movers going in and out of the house with boxes and furniture. But no Jocelyn.

He burst inside, probably looking like a crazy person. When one mover handed him a box, he tried to explain he wasn't one of them, but the words came out all jumbled.

"I'm not—no, stop handing me boxes—I'm the husband!"

His words were muffled when another box was added on top of the one that had been shoved at him.

"Congrats, dude. We're all husbands here. Doesn't mean you can't pick up a box," the mover groused.

Luke dutifully took the boxes to the truck, knowing he was losing precious time. When he returned inside, he slipped past the taskmaster mover to find Jocelyn. Even Fluffer would work at this point.

He didn't find either sister, or the rabbit, but he did find his father-in-law in a small bedroom. He was sitting on a bed that was stripped of sheets and pillows. He was staring at a framed photo.

"Mr. Gray?" said Luke.

"Who's asking?"

"I'm Luke. Jocelyn's husband."

Pete gave him a brief glance before narrowing his eyes. "What are you doing here?"

"I'm looking for Jocelyn."

"Too little, too late for that, son."

"If you could just tell me where she is—"

"She's gone. She left in a taxi for the ferry."

Luke's heart twisted. "Shit. I have to find her."

Now Pete looked suspicious. "Why? Because you've already done enough. You broke her heart in two. If I were ten years younger, I'd break your head in."

"And I'd deserve it. You're welcome to do it later. But first I need to find Jocelyn."

Pete rose, setting the photo aside. He stood toe-to-toe with Luke, his gaze hard. Although he had the look of a man whose body was deteriorating, he didn't give off an air of weakness, either.

"Tell me what you want with my daughter," said Pete.

"I love her. I fuck—screwed up. Badly. I know I did. I need to tell her that."

"You know, when I found out she married you, I wasn't happy about it. I knew she did it to help me, and I hated that. But I've also learned that sometimes you have to ask for help. Jocelyn isn't good about doing that. She's too much like me. She needs somebody who will take care of her, make her slow down every once in a while. Are you that guy?"

"I am. Your daughter—she's amazing. She's the

strongest person I've ever met. She makes me want to be a better man."

Pete assessed him further, then nodded. "Go after her then. Can't say I give you my approval, but that's for Jocelyn to decide. Not me."

Luke, in a burst of relief, hugged his father-in-law. He returned the hug with a chuckle.

Luke drove to the ferry terminal so fast that he must've run a red light or two. He kept looking at his watch. When he finally parked, it was after one o'clock, and the ferry had just departed.

"Shit. Shit!" Luke watched the ferry slowly sail into the distance, and he could've sunk to his knees in despair.

Not knowing what else to do, he wandered into the ferry terminal and sat down on a bench. He might as well get a ticket for the next ferry, he figured. Maybe he could catch up with Jocelyn at the airport.

"Luke?"

Luke raised his head to see his wife standing in front of him. The sun shone in a halo behind her head, making her blond hair glow golden. She looked thinner, with dark circles under her eyes. Despite that, she was the most beautiful thing he'd seen in ages.

"Jocelyn. I thought you were on the ferry."

"I was running late and missed the one at one o'clock." She had her arms crossed, her expression tense. "Are you going somewhere?"

"I was looking for you."

She blinked. "Oh."

He got up, but he kept some distance between them. She looked so closed off that his heart ached.

"Tristan told me what he did. That he told you to let me go."

Now she was studiously looking everywhere but at him. "He didn't convince me. I just knew it's better this way."

"No. It's not better. Jocelyn, look at me. Please."

She raised her eyes.

"I love you. I was an asshole. I think I was too afraid to believe that this marriage we'd done so impulsively could turn out to be something real. I don't care about the money. I know you wanted to help your dad. I can't blame you for that—"

"God, Luke, just shut up." Jocelyn was crying now, her cheeks red. "You think you can just show up here and tell me you're sorry and everything is forgotten?"

He got down on one knee and took her hands.

"People are staring," she hissed.

"Let them stare." He looked at their audience, which consisted of all of four people. "I love this woman! I love her more than anything!" he proclaimed to the crowd.

One woman tittered. A janitor just shook his head and continued mopping in front of the restrooms.

"Luke, get up." Jocelyn sighed. "You don't have to do this."

He got up, but he didn't let go of her hands. "If I have to spend every day proving that I love you, I will. Because you're worth the effort. Jocelyn, you're everything. You're the woman of my dreams. Don't you know that? Ever since we were teenagers, when we first became friends. I loved you then, I think. Let me love you, baby."

Tears overflowed down her cheeks. She tried wiping them away, but they kept coming. "I love you, too," she whispered. "You piss me off and frustrate me, and yet at the same time you're such a kind, giving, amazing man. It's obnoxious."

He laughed. "So you're staying here? With me?"

At that question, her eyes widened. "Oh. I'm going to San Francisco. I got a job."

"I know." He stepped closer. "If you want to go, I'll go with you. I'll go with you wherever you want."

"Even the Arctic Circle?" She smiled.

"I'll live in an ice castle with you if you want. But I draw the line at getting a pet polar bear."

"That sounds reasonable."

Luke had his arm around her now. As he was about to kiss her, a woman yelled, "Kiss her already!"

Jocelyn spluttered out a laugh, which Luke silenced with a kiss. The ferry terminal crowd burst into applause. When they ended the kiss, they were both red-faced and smiling like idiots.

"I want to stay," murmured Jocelyn. "I don't want to leave the island."

"Are you sure?"

"There will be other jobs. But leaving my friends and family behind? I'm not ready for that yet. Besides, Gwen needs me."

"And I need you."

"Well, that's a given." She smiled, but the smile faded as she asked, "What about the divorce papers?"

"Oh, those? I tore them up. I hope you don't mind."

"Thank God. Because I was going to ask to burn them otherwise."

Luke touched his nose to hers. "Let's go home." He

reached down to pick up the pet carrier that contained Fluffer. "Guess you're coming with us, buddy."

"He missed you."

Considering Fluffer looked about as excited as he always did—not enthused at all—Luke wasn't so sure. But he didn't mind. As long as he had his beloved wife, she could own as many taciturn rabbits her heart desired.

EPILOGUE

"Coming in your wedding clothes seems a bit on the nose, doesn't it?" Opal blew out a puff of smoke as she took in Luke and Jocelyn's appearance.

"You were invited to the wedding. Again," replied Luke.

"I already saw the first one. I don't need to see the second one. Weddings are all the same, at any rate. You've seen one, you've seen them all," said Opal.

Jocelyn, wearing a white dress that was so fluffy that she felt like she was wearing a cloud, had to restrain a laugh. When Luke had told her a week ago that Opal wanted to meet right before their wedding, she hadn't even been surprised.

Nothing about their life together was surprising at this point. After a year together, the only thing that was surprising to Jocelyn was the fact that every day seemed to bring more happiness. More laughter, more love. She couldn't have dreamed a more perfect marriage.

"Well, renewing your vows or whatever it is you're doing is one way to show that you're in love," said Opal. She glanced around the room inside the small church where Jocelyn and Luke would stand up soon. "Having a traditional church wedding seems out of character."

"My mom suggested it," replied Luke.

"Huh." Opal stubbed out her cigarette.

Despite it being the middle of summer, she wore her usual furs along with strings of pearls. She seemed incapable of being too warm, though. Jocelyn didn't notice a single drop of sweat on the woman's face.

"When I got home, I heard that you two had broken up. I even heard that there may have been divorce papers drawn up." Opal raised an eyebrow. "True?"

Jocelyn looked at Luke. Luke replied, "True, but they were never signed."

"Not exactly a great testament to you two being in love. Are you going to file for divorce six months from now?"

Jocelyn touched Luke's arm to keep him for retorting something rude. "We've already been married for over a year now. We bought a house together. We even have a second rabbit, and we plan to start a family eventually. Altogether, doesn't it seem like we're the real deal?"

Luke squeezed her hand. "I love her. I love you," he added, looking at Jocelyn. "She makes me get up in the morning. She makes me excited for the future."

"Luke makes me want to be nice to people," added Jocelyn, only semi-joking.

"I'm not going to lie and say it's been easy. We've had issues we've had to work out. But we're still here. We still like each other—love each other. Isn't that what really matters?" said Luke passionately.

"I love you," said Jocelyn softly.

To Jocelyn's surprise, Opal smiled at them. It was a bright, genuine smile, a look neither of them had ever seen on her face. Then she got up, took both of their faces, and kissed first one cheek, then the other.

"Oh, I can't tell you how happy this makes me. I wanted to believe you two were meant to be, and I was right. Love found a way to keep you two together."

Jocelyn gaped. Was Opal tearing up?

"Are you telling us you're a romantic?" said Luke.

"Always have been. Why do you think your grandma chose me? But I had to make it seem like I was coldhearted. I didn't want to make things too easy."

Jocelyn stared at Luke. Luke stared back, then shrugged a single shoulder.

"We don't need the money," he said, "so it's your choice if we're going to get it or not. Even if we don't get a cent, I'll never let Jocelyn go."

Opal beamed. "How lovely." She dabbed at her eyes with a handkerchief. "Now, get out of here. Go get married again. I'll deal with the paperwork."

The wedding went off without a hitch. The contrast between this ceremony and their first was stark. Instead of feeling like she was walking to her doom, Jocelyn felt only pure joy, walking with her dad toward Luke.

Pete was crying when he handed Luke his daughter's hand. "Take care of her," he said roughly.

"I will." Luke's words were filled with resolve.

There wasn't a dry eye in the church when they said their vows. By the time they were pronounced to be husband and wife again, Jocelyn had already gone through multiple tissues. She was just glad Alex had thought to bring a bunch with her down the aisle.

They held the reception at Lyn's, although Gwen had forbidden Jocelyn from cooking anything. Jocelyn's new sous chef, Naomi, had been the one in charge. Naomi had been a breath of fresh air ever since Jocelyn had hired her to replace Kelly. And to Jocelyn's delight, the food she'd made was exquisite.

Sitting at the head table with her husband and bridal party, Jocelyn couldn't remember being so happy. Bekah, her matron of honor, leaned toward her to say, "Congratulations, again. I'm so happy for you two."

Bekah was holding her one-year-old daughter Marian. Her older daughter was dancing with her dad at the moment. Marian cooed and reached for Jocelyn.

"You and Elliot make some cute babies," said Jocelyn.

"Aren't they? I know every parent is supposed to say that, but they are pretty darn cute."

Marian became fascinated with Jocelyn's necklace, which she then proceeded to try to chew on. Jocelyn handed the baby back, albeit reluctantly.

Jocelyn had never experienced baby fever until recently. Maybe it'd been because of Bekah's kids. Or maybe it was just because she wanted to have a family with Luke finally.

"You look like you're thinking about something," said Bekah.

"I just never thought I'd be here. Married, in love. Thinking about having kids. I always thought I'd just be married to my career."

"Well, I get that. I was always afraid I could only ever

have one or the other, not both. But you can have both. You can have it all."

Jocelyn smiled as she watched Luke approach her. His answering smile made her heart lift. "I know. Isn't it great?"

ALEX GRAY LOVED WEDDINGS. Part of it was because it was a day to get dressed up and be admired, but the other part was because they were so romantic. She loved watching couples say their vows. The first dances, the cake cutting. She'd always dreamed of having that for herself. More and more, though, she wasn't sure she'd ever get it.

Her last relationship had lasted all of six months. She hadn't even been that upset when she'd broken up with the guy. More often than not, Alex found herself getting bored in relationships. It was as if guys simply couldn't keep up with her. When she wanted to run, they just wanted to walk leisurely

Nobody wanted to have adventures or do something daring. Nobody wanted to take a risk. Alex wanted a man with whom she could take risks.

Alex smiled as she watched her sister dance with her husband. But despite her best efforts, the green snake of jealousy circled around her heart.

Where was her knight in shining armor?

While people danced and partied, Alex slipped outside. It was the perfect summer evening with clear skies. She inhaled the sea air, closing her eyes.

"Where are you?" she whispered into the wind. It didn't

help that Hazel Island was so small. There weren't exactly a lot of eligible bachelors available to date.

Maybe she should give up, sell the bookstore, and move somewhere else. But she couldn't—not yet. She couldn't let the bookstore go, not when she'd poured so much heart and soul into it.

The restaurant wasn't far from the ocean. Alex wandered toward the beach. Although there were still people walking around, there were fewer nearer to the water.

Alex figured that she wouldn't be missed for a few minutes. She just wanted to settle her thoughts. She figured her sister would understand.

She was startled out of her reverie by the sound of footsteps. A man approached. With his face in shadows, she couldn't tell who it was.

He stopped when he noticed her. They stared at each other, both of them flummoxed at seeing another human being down by the water at night.

"I didn't think anyone else would be down here," the man said.

"It is a public beach," Alex pointed out.

He chuckled. "Fair enough." He stepped closer to Alex until she could make out his face. He was a stranger to her. He was tall and was lightly bearded, his hair a little shaggy but not unkempt. When he turned his face toward the moonlight, she saw that his eyes were a pale blue. Where had this handsome man appeared from?

"Did you come for the wedding?" she asked. Maybe he was a friend of Luke's, she thought.

"The wedding?" He raised his eyebrows. "Is that why you're dressed like that?"

Alex looked down at her attire. "What, in a dress?"

"A flimsy little thing that looks like you'd freeze, yeah."

"Are you concerned I'm going to catch a chill?" Alex joked.

The man was so close that Alex could've reached out and touched him. She suddenly realized that she was all alone with a strange man. If she were smart, she'd head back to the restaurant.

She couldn't tell if he was dressed for a wedding or just in usual business attire. But who would be getting home from work at eight p.m. on a Saturday night?

To her surprise, he shrugged out of his suit jacket and placed it around her. "So you don't freeze," he said roughly.

She inhaled the scent of his jacket—something woodsy and spicy—and found that she didn't have any snappy remarks to make. Her heart was pounding, and she could feel excitement build inside her.

Was this the adventure she'd been searching for?

"What's your name?" asked Alex.

The man smiled. "You first."

"I'm Alex." She gave him a playful curtsy. "I'm the bride's sister."

"But not her maid of honor."

So he *had* been at the wedding. "Our relationship is complicated. Not that it's any of your business, though. She asked me if I wanted to be her maid of honor and I said no. I knew I wouldn't have enough time to dedicate to helping her as she deserved."

"That's very selfless of you."

Alex raised her chin. "You're making fun of me."

"Never."

He stepped so close that Alex felt his breath puff against her face. He was nearly a head taller than her. She had to tilt her head back to see his eyes.

When he leaned down and kissed her, giddiness filled her. The kiss started soft, almost unsure, but soon it turned into a heated embrace that made Alex's head spin.

Then it was over. It took Alex a moment to come back to earth.

"Have a good night, Alex," the man said.

"Wait! Your jacket!"

He glanced over his shoulder. "Keep it. Something to remember me by."

ABOUT THE AUTHOR

A coffee addict and cat lover, USA Today bestselling author Iris Morland writes sparkling, swoon-worthy romances, including the Flower Shop Sisters and the Love Everlasting series.

If she's not reading or writing, she enjoys binging on Netflix shows and cooking something delicious.

She currently lives in Seattle with her partner, two cats, and an excessive number of houseplants.

www.ingramcontent.com/pod-product-compliance
Lightning Source LLC
Chambersburg PA
CBHW050844190726
48286CB00007B/2221